Bobby's Story

Written by
J. Richard Knapp

Illustration by Melissa Roberts

Proudly Published in the USA by
Thornton Publishing, Inc
17011 Lincoln Ave. #408
Parker, CO 80134

Phone: (303)-794-8888
Fax: (720)-863-2013

www.BooksToBelieveIn.com/BobbysStory.php

www.ProfitablePublishing.net
publisher@profitablepublishing.net

ISBN: 0-9774761-7-0

Dedication

It is estimated that nearly a third of all youths in our country have been a bully, the target of a bully, or both. It is national problem in our young people that must be recognized and dealt with. <u>Bobby's Story</u> is dedicated to all the people who have endured the ugliness of a bully and the long lasting images left in our memories.

The recall of these cruelties could not have been possible without the support and encouragement of my wife, Barbara: my children, Cathy, Heather, Christie, Rick; and my granddaughter, Makayla.

Lastly, this book is dedicated to Tim, who understands the true power of just one person, and the difference a person can make in the lives of others.

~*J. Richard Knapp*

Contents

CHAPTER 1

Something Beautiful

Tiny white puffs of air appeared from the faces of the boys and girls as they walked to school. The morning frost covered the ground with an icy white blanket - a cold gust of winter wind sent a chill up their backs. The students looked up into the gray sky for the first signs of snow and zipped their coats up a little closer to their chins.

Stephanie, Maria, and Whitney giggled as they walked down the sidewalk together - sharing their most recent gossip. They were well known for spreading rumors and saying cruel things about the other students. Most students tried to avoid them. Some students acted like they were their friends, so as not to get picked on.

The three girls started up the stairs toward the giant front doors of the school. Whitney was telling her usual gossip about everyone to Stephanie and Maria.

Maria interrupted Whitney's story and pointed to a boy standing by the door. She bobbed her head side to side and looked at the boy in disgust. "Who is that?" Maria stepped slightly toward the boy, as if examining him. "He looks so – poor!" Maria moved back and leaned against Stephanie and Whitney, as if she were getting too close to the boy. "Do you think he's contagious?" The girls laughed at Maria's cruel comment.

Whitney covered her mouth with her hand and spoke softly to Maria and Stephanie, but loud enough for the boy to hear. "He moved here this week. His name is Bobby something." Whitney continued to make fun of the boy. "He's really strange and rarely talks to anyone."

Maria reached out slowly with her hand – pointing at Bobby with her finger. "Look at those – those old clothes!" She leaned forward over her arm, as if she were aiming her finger at the boy's chest. "His coat is so big - it must have been used for a tent." She pulled her finger back and smiled at Whitney and Stephanie.

Whitney began to laugh softly, as she motioned Maria and Stephanie to go on inside the building. The girls broke into a loud laughter once they were inside. They made sure Bobby could hear them.

Bobby stared at the ground ignoring the mean comments and laughter of the girls. His long curly brown hair hung down over his forehead. A small tear began to build up in the corner of each eye, as he continued to look down at his feet. Bobby watched sadly as the first of several glistening teardrops fell to his feet. He wiped the next set of tears from his eyes with his old worn out coat, pulled his hands back up the sleeves, and crossed his arms to keep the cold air out.

The boy moved closer to the door awaiting the morning bell. Bobby moved his feet back and forth slowly, revealing two old worn out summer shoes with small holes near the toes and on the sides.

Students walked by Bobby one after another or in small groups. None of them looked his way or even said hello.

Bobby continued to look down at the ground, as he tried to stay warm.

"Good morning." A tall man with graying hair stood in front of Bobby. He had seen the girls talking to the boy, and figured they were being rude to him. "Are you okay, son?"

Bobby looked up slowly at the tall man. He recognized him as Mr. Roberts, the science teacher, and nodded his head. "I'm okay." Bobby's voice was without emotion, as he looked into the concerned face of the teacher, and then looked back down at his feet.

Mr. Roberts studied the boy more closely. "What is your name?"

The boy looked back up into the eyes of the teacher. "Bobby."

"You're new – aren't you?" Mr. Roberts continued to examine Bobby.

"Yes," Bobby seemed very nervous, "we moved here this week."

"You're going to be in my science class starting today. I'm glad to meet you." Mr. Roberts continued to look carefully at Bobby's nervous face. "You have a good day. I will see you after lunch." The teacher turned away from the boy and continued down the sidewalk for a short distance. Mr. Roberts stopped and turned around to look at Bobby by the door one more time. He watched as

Bobby huddled up in his coat again and stared at his feet as other students walked by him into the building. Mr. Roberts turned back around and continued on his way down the sidewalk.

A loud bell broke the morning silence and signaled a warning that classes would begin in five minutes. Soon, there were no students left outside. Bobby's eyes slowly looked up and around him. He cautiously slipped inside the doorway, looking down each direction of the hallway. Most of the students were already into their classrooms. Here and there a student hurried to get into a room before the tardy bell.

Bobby stood just inside the main doors for a moment. He didn't want to walk into his classroom until the last second - it was a way for him to avoid the other students and teachers.

His dark eyes were searching for a quiet place to hide for just a few more minutes. He saw the perfect place across the hallway from him – a boy's bathroom. Bobby moved quickly into the bathroom. His eyes looked in each direction of the room to see if any students were in there – he saw no one.

Bobby figured it was a safe place to be alone. He stood in the middle of the room staring at the beautiful dark blue tiles on the wall surrounding the mirrors. Bobby looked at himself in one of the mirrors – it reminded him of a picture in a beautiful blue frame. He gazed at his messed up hair and tried to comb it as best he could with his fingers. Bobby thought to himself as he ran his fingers through his hair, "Curls! Why couldn't my hair have been straight?" Bobby moved his curly hair away from his eyes.

The bathroom door slammed opened. "OUT OF MY WAY JERK!" shouted the voice.

A hand hit Bobby in the shoulder - knocking him off balance. He fell hard against the side of the sink and crumpled to the floor. His eyes looked up to see a tall red haired boy with freckles looking down at him laughing hard.

A shorter boy with blonde hair stood beside the boy laughing. The blonde looked at the red haired bully, and then at Bobby sitting on the floor with all his things scattered around him. He didn't laugh at first, but did so very quickly when the red haired bully looked at him. The boy began to laugh quickly. It was obvious that he did not want the red haired bully to get angry with him.

The bully kicked one of Bobby's books across the room, then picked up another one and threw it at a toilet nearby. Luckily, it missed and landed on the floor. The bully held up his flat out stretched hand high in the air, as he walked toward his blonde friend by the bathroom door. They slapped hands high in the air, and then walked out of the bathroom together.

The blonde boy looked back at Bobby one last time before the door closed. He was relieved the red haired boy was picking on this new kid - instead of him!

Bobby remained on the floor and stared at the boys until they disappeared through the doorway. He struggled back up to his feet and looked at himself in the mirror – fighting back the tears forming in the corners of his eyes. "Why do I have to be in this stupid school?" Bobby kicked into the air and threw his elbows around angrily. "I want to go back home!" He placed both hands on the edges of the sink and looked unhappily at himself in the mirror with tears slowly trickling down his cheeks into the sink.

Bobby tried to remember a day long ago when his life was happy and fun. He continued to look at his miserable face in the mirror, wondering why all these dreadful things were happening to him now.

After a few quiet moments, Bobby began to pick up his things scattered on the floor. He carefully placed a book of dinosaurs on the edge of the sink and turned the pages to a picture of a terrifying Tyrannosaurus Rex. "I wished you'd have been here a couple of minutes ago."

He stared at the picture for several seconds trying to imagine the red haired boy running for his life down the hallway with Tyrannosaurus Rex right behind him trying to bite his rear. A slight smile formed in the corners of Bobby's mouth, as he thought about it. "Maybe, T Rex could invite you to breakfast!" The boy looked around the room for more of his things. He needed to hurry – the tardy bell would ring soon.

Bobby placed his second book about rockets on top of the dinosaur book. His mind continued to think of funny things for the bully and his blonde friend, "I wonder what would happen if we sent the red-haired boy to the moon on a rocket," Bobby chuckled, "with T Rex as his co-pilot!" He pictured the red haired boy in a space suit trying to out run the dinosaur inside a rocket, "He'd probably feed his blonde friend to T Rex first!"

Bobby remembered the book near the toilet. It was not one of his books from school. He walked over to the old book on the floor, picked it up, and looked it over carefully to make sure it wasn't damaged. The book appeared to be very old. Bobby opened the cover of the book to a hand written note on the page. 'Merry Christmas Bobby! Love Grandma.'

Bobby felt the sadness returning to his heart again. He remembered his grandmother giving him the book at Christmas last year. His mind wistfully pictured the entire family singing songs, eating cakes and cookies, and opening presents by the giant fireplace.

The boy felt a choking inside him, as he tried to breathe. He wanted so very badly to go back home to his family and friends.

Bobby took off his old worn out coat and placed it under his arm, and then picked up the books on the edge of the sink with his other hand. Bobby hurried, as he knew the tardy bell was about to ring. He turned to look at himself in the mirror for one last time, and then walked out the doorway to his classroom.

Mr. Reed, an English teacher, stood at the front of the room, erasing the work on the chalkboard from the day before. He was a stocky man with dark brown hair and glasses that matched. The teacher always wore a white shirt and tie – most of his ties were usually bright colors and strange designs which did not match his clothes.

The teacher always seemed to have a look of seriousness about him. He saw the classroom door opening slowly to his right and turned to look more carefully. His eyes made contact with Bobby, as he walked through the doorway. Mr. Reed looked down at his watch and back at Bobby again. "You're timing it pretty close." The teacher turned back around and continued cleaning the chalkboard.

It appeared most of the students were already in their seats or visiting with friends nearby. None of them paid attention to Bobby trying to sneak unnoticed to the back of the room.

Bobby walked down the aisle beside the wall with his eyes to the floor - never looking at the students, as he passed by. He slid quietly into a desk near the back of the room, took a spiral notebook and pencil from his backpack, and placed them beside his books on the top of the desk. He glanced quickly around the room – no one seemed to pay attention to him. Bobby's dark brown eyes looked back down at his desktop; and began writing on a page in his spiral notebook.

For a moment, he stopped writing to think about his next sentence. At that exact moment, his notebook and the books exploded off the desk toward the wall! Bobby's eyes focused on a freckled hand flying across his desk where the books had once been. His eyes followed the freckled hand upward. It was the tall red hair boy standing there grinning down at him. "Oops! Sorry about that!"

Bobby watched in disbelief as the red haired boy walked up the aisle a couple of desks and sat down. He wanted to run out the door of the room, but his body remained frozen to the chair. Just breathing air seemed hard!

The blonde boy with the bully in the bathroom was seated across from the red haired boy. "Give me five!" said the bully. The red haired boy slapped his friend's hand hard, and then the bully looked back at Bobby with a big grin on his face. The other students in the area ducked their heads, trying not to laugh, or so it seemed.

Mr. Reed turned around at the sound of the books hitting the floor, but saw nothing. He stared at the bully for a moment, and then looked down at some papers on his desk.

Bobby felt the air coming back into his lungs and looked back down at the floor sadly. He slipped quietly out of his desk and began to pick his things up. The students near him watched – but no one helped him.

"Here's your pencil." A voice whispered to him from behind. "Don't mind him. Big head – tiny brain!" The boy gave Bobby a quick smile. "I'm Tim."

Bobby looked into the smiling face of a small skinny boy wearing black rimmed glasses. The lenses were so thick, that his dark-blue eyes looked big and round. Bobby noticed the boy's light brown hair was a mess – in fact – his whole body was a mess. Tim's shirt was buttoned crooked, and his pants and shoes had mud on them. Bobby glanced at Tim's things on his desk. They were a mess also. Bobby couldn't help but smile back at this messy kid with a great sense of humor. "Thanks. I'm Bobby."

Bobby took the pencil from Tim and placed it on his desk. He continued searching the floor to look for his notebook, but couldn't see it. His eyes came to stop, as he saw the feet of Mr. Reed standing in front of him. Bobby looked up slowly. The teacher stood there like a giant tree in front of him with the notebook open in his big hands – he was reading each word of Bobby's writing very carefully.

"Not bad!" said Mr. Reed. He placed a hand on Bobby's shoulder and set the notebook back on his desk. "Pretty good stuff. I like your writing style."

Tim tried to look over Bobby's shoulder at the notebook, but Bobby closed it quickly and placed his hands on it.

Mr. Reed walked back up the aisle to the front of the room. He stopped by the red hair boy's desk for just a moment and stared deep into his eyes. "Your life is about to make a dramatic change."

The red hair boy acted as if he had no idea what the teacher was talking about. He waited until Mr. Reed turned his back then stuck his tongue out at him. A few students nearby giggled. The teacher turned around, only to see the boy acting as if nothing was happening.

Bobby eased back into his desk and opened his notebook. He looked around the room one time to make sure no one else was going to have an 'oops' again with his things. His eyes glanced quickly up the aisle to make sure the red haired boy and his buddy were still in their seats. Bobby noticed some of the students staring at him. He quickly looked back down at his notebook and began writing in it again.

The final bell rang which meant the starting of class. All of the students stood up in the room at the same time and began to say the Pledge of Allegiance. It was a daily occurrence in the classroom. The students sat back down quietly in their seats and listened to the morning announcements being read over the school loud speaker. Bobby figured it was probably a secretary in the office reading out loud into a microphone. He continued to look down at his notebook and write in it as the announcements went on.

There was a silence after the announcements. It seemed to last several minutes. The students looked at each other nervously. Finally, Mr. Reed, who was seated at his desk, pushed his chair back. He stood up slowly and moved to the front of the classroom. His eyes looked slowly from one student to the next. The teacher watched the nervousness in each of them. It was clear to everyone in the room something was wrong. His eyes stopped and focused on the red hair boy. Many of the students followed the eyes of the teacher to the bully. Once they realized it was about the red haired boy, they quickly looked back down at their desks.

After a few seconds, the teacher calmly directed the class to take out their homework and pass it to the front of the classroom. Mr. Reed watched carefully as each student in the room passed their assignments to the person in front of them. The red hair boy smiled to his blonde friend, as he placed his paper on the stack. It was obvious that they were up to something.

The teacher saw the two boys smiling at each other. The expression on his face remained unchanged. He walked to the first person in each row and picked up the papers.

Mr. Reed stood at the front of the classroom skimming through the papers. The teacher looked at the front side of each page, and then turn it over, looking at the other side carefully. He examined one paper very carefully. Then, his eyes looked up slowly and fixed on the tall red hair boy's face. "Johnny. Come here!" The students in the room seemed to hold their breath all at once. There was an utterly complete silence everywhere in classroom. Each student watched with wide eyes! They knew big trouble was about to begin.

An ugly scowl slowly formed on Johnny's face. "Why? I didn't do anything." The bully continued to scowl as he slipped out of his desk and walked to the front of the room. He looked down at many of the students, as he walked by them with a strut and threatening sneer.

"Did you have much trouble with your assignment last night?" Mr. Reed continued to look down at the paper. His eyes were clearly focused on the second page of the assignment.

"No. It was pretty easy." Johnny grinned as he glanced toward his blonde buddy, Brad. No one laughed at his humor or even smiled. The class was convinced that Johnny was in trouble for something.

"Would you mind explaining for me and the rest of the class the answer to number three?" Mr.

Reed's eyes lifted slowly from the paper and began to stare at Johnny.

Johnny's face turned red. "Uh! I forgot which one that was."

"I'm surprised - considering there were only four questions on this assignment." Mr. Reed watched as the red hair boy's eyes darted back and forth. "There were two questions on the front page and only two questions on the back page. I want you to tell me about question number three." The teacher continued to stare deeply into Johnny's eyes, watching his nervousness growing. "That is the first question on the back of the front page."

A small red splotch suddenly appeared under Johnny's chin on his freckled throat. The students in the room began to notice the red spot getting bigger and bigger. Students were nudging each other and bringing it to their attention, but careful not to say anything out loud. They watched, as the spot grew larger and larger - soon it went all the way around the red haired boy's neck and up his face.

A voice broke the silence of the room. "Whoa!" All eyes in the classroom looked in the direction of Bobby at the rear of the room – including Johnny! They were all thinking the same thought, "How could anyone be so stupid?"

Bobby had that look on his face that said, "I didn't do it!"

The teacher stepped toward Johnny. "Let me repeat it again. I want you to explain the answer to the third question." He handed the paper back to Johnny. "Maybe this will help your memory."

More splotches appeared on Johnny's face and neck. He turned from pink to a dark red color - as he tried to explain the answer on the page. Instead, Johnny just made a lot of nonsense statements. Finally, he turned to the teacher, "I don't remember how I did this."

"Did anyone help you with this assignment?" The teacher's eyes continued to stare hard at Johnny. "Brad! Did you help him?"

Brad answered quickly, "No sir! I didn't even finish the assignment. I had no clue what to do." Brad shook his head wondering what had made him say such a stupid thing. He heard a few soft giggles around him. Brad looked slowly downward to the floor, as he knew Johnny was staring at him angrily.

Mr. Reed thumbed through the papers until he found Brad's. He looked over the assignment very carefully. "I can see you are right."

Brad breathed a sigh of relief. He didn't want any part of the trouble Johnny was in.

"And seeing how you have no clue of what the answer is; I think you should see me after school for some extra help – say for about an extra hour!" The teacher watched as Brad slumped down in his chair. "I will give your mom a call so she doesn't worry about you."

"Great! I'll get grounded for a month." Brad just kept sliding further down in his chair. "I'll probably get blamed for..."

Johnny gave Brad a threatening look. Brad knew he had better shut up.

Mr. Reed watched Brad's reaction, and then

fixed his attention back on Johnny. "Has your memory returned yet?"

Johnny tried to think as fast as he could, "Nope! It just went blank." He tried to sneak in a smile for the students behind him. No one laughed. They just kept staring at the red splotches on his face and neck.

The teacher continued to stare at Johnny. "Maybe that's because this is not your work!"

"I didn't cheat!" shouted Johnny. The dark red splotches on his face suddenly turned pure white. Even his freckles were losing their orange color. The students in the class were totally amazed by the changes in Johnny's skin.

Tim whispered in Bobby's ear, "The guy is changing colors like a chameleon."

Bobby had to look at the wall so he wouldn't laugh - it wasn't working. He felt a laugh moving its way up from his stomach slowly to his throat. He tried to force it back down, but failed. The silence of the classroom was broken as Bobby tried to cover up the laugh with a cough. The students in the classroom turned toward him, wondering what his half laugh and half cough was. Again, they couldn't believe this new kid was so stupid.

Mr. Reed glanced quickly a Bobby for a moment, then back at Johnny. A smile slowly crept across the face of the teacher. "I changed the third question for the afternoon class. You answered that question – not yours." The teacher watched the reality of getting caught enter the brain of Johnny. "The next time you choose to steal someone's work, make sure they have the same assignment as you. Go to the Principal's Office!"

Johnny picked up his books and other things angrily, and then walked toward the door.

A muffled laugh came from the back corner of the classroom again. Every student in the room, including Johnny, looked at Bobby. His dark brown eyes immediately looked back down at the notebook in his hands.

Johnny stopped at the door and gave Bobby a threatening stare as he left the room. Everyone knew that look meant trouble for the new kid.

Tim leaned forward in his desk and whispered to Bobby, "You'd better watch out for him. I've seen that look before."

Bobby continued to ignore Tim and the other students. He heard a girl across the aisle whisper to another girl, "The new kid is going to get it. Did you see the look on Johnny's face? I wouldn't want to be that kid."

Soon, the students all over the classroom were whispering. This would be the biggest gossip of the day.

Mr. Reed broke the sound of whispers in the room with his loud voice. "I would suggest that each of you remember to get your homework done on time and on your own." His eyes looked one more time at Brad. "Take out your journals. I want you to describe something very beautiful that you have seen or experienced. Each of you will share your work with the rest of the class in thirty minutes."

Many of the students looked at each other, and wondered what to write about. Some students started writing almost immediately. Bobby looked down at his blank paper and closed his eyes for a few moments. He opened his eyes and began writing. Bobby never looked up as he wrote sentence after sentence on the paper.

Mr. Reed's voice broke the silence. "Let's share your work with the rest of the class." Mr. Reed looked at his class list of student names. "Susan! You're first."

A small girl on the far side of the room stood up and faced the class. "My family went to a national park last summer in Wyoming. There was a mountain behind a lake that was very beautiful. Each morning, we would look at the reflection of the mountain on the still water. It was really pretty."

"Great job, Susan!" stated Mr. Reed loudly. "Please close your eyes." He watched as Susan closed her eyes. "Can you picture the mountain in your mind?" His voice changed from serious to calming. It was obvious to the students; the teacher was trying to assure Susan that she could do it.

"Yes," said Susan shyly.

Mr. Reed went on, "I want you to describe the mountain."

Susan looked cautiously around the room, and then back at the teacher. "The mountain is high with jagged rocks. The sides of the rocky mountain look pink – I think it is because the sun is rising." She paused for a moment. "There is a small amount of snow on the top of the mountain and in one of the valleys. It looks dirty – not like fresh snow." She opened her eyes slowly and looked at the teacher.

"You did a great job Susan," said Mr. Reed. Susan sat down in her seat again with a big grin on her face. A couple of students smiled and gave her some words of encouragement.

Mr. Reed looked to the center of the room. "Maria. How about you? What did you find beautiful?" The teacher sat down on the corner of his desk to listen.

"Gossip!" said a voice from the side of the room. A soft whispered laughter went around the room quickly. Many students looked at each other with smiles on their faces.

Maria stood up and stuck her tongue out at the students laughing. "I think shopping for a new dress at the mall is absolutely beautiful – just look at this. I got this one yesterday." Maria turned around slowly showing everyone her new dress. "There is not another one like it." Maria lifted her nose up into the air and sat down.

"Lucky for us!" said a voice by the wall. All eyes in the room looked toward Bobby and Tim. Bobby continued to look down at his notebook. Tim acted as if nothing had happened.

Maria scrunched her lips together and tilted her head sideways. She figured it was that 'smart aleck' Tim making fun of her again.

Bobby looked up slowly into the face of Maria. Instead of saying anything, he just smiled and looked back at his notebook. He was thinking about her comments outside with Whitney and Stephanie. He drew a quick picture of T Rex chasing a girl. He glanced back at Maria and smiled even bigger.

Maria couldn't handle the last smile from Bobby – much less Tim making faces at her. She scrunched her lips again, threw her hair back, and looked back down at her notes.

"That's enough." The teacher waited for the class to quiet down again. "Maria. It's your turn. Close your eyes and describe the dress."

Maria tried to get one last look at her dress.

"Close your eyes," reminded Mr. Reed. "Describe the dress."

"It – it's brown." The students watched, as Maria struggled to describe the dress she was wearing. "It has some flowers on it – I think." Maria's face turned a deep red. "It's expensive and that's all that matters."

All of the students stared in disbelief as Maria sat down. They had now seen two students changing colors in class today! Nobody said a word - not even Mr. Reed.

"Well," said Maria one last time. "It is very expensive!" Her eyes turned toward Bobby. "At least my family can afford clothes!" Maria's words flew across the room like a dagger into Bobby's heart. The other students listened in disbelief, but said nothing.

Bobby's dark brown eyes stared back at the girl through his curls. He fought back the tears and said nothing. Bobby looked down at his notebook again. A few teardrops fell on the page he was writing on. The ink on the page turned into little blue puddles. Bobby realized some of his words had been ruined. He turned his face toward the wall away from the students and Maria.

"Lay off him." Tim's voice broke the silence. "It was me – not him." He stared at Maria waiting for her to say something again.

Maria's head bobbled back and forth a couple of times. "As if anyone cares?"

"Tim-" Mr. Reed interrupted the two. "Why don't you tell us what you find beautiful?"

Tim stood up behind Bobby. "I think my socks are the most beautiful thing in the world." Tim stood there with a huge grin on his face looking at the class. There was a moment of silence in the room - then the entire class broke into laughter. Bobby turned back around and began to smile.

"Tim!" Mr. Reed tried to regain control of the class.

"It's the truth!" stated Tim, as he looked proudly around the room. "I wore these socks at my first baseball game last summer. I hit a homerun on the very first pitch." He pulled up his pant legs to reveal two very – very – very dirty socks underneath. "I haven't taken them off even once since then." He started to untie his shoes. "Here, I'll show you."

Mr. Reed stepped forward. "No! We'll take your word for it." … But it was already too late. Tim had one shoe off and was adjusting the dirty sock.

The teacher stepped back as the smell was beginning to spread across the room. Students were hiding their faces and gagging. It was a disgusting smell.

"Put your shoe back on!" Mr. Reed shook his head, "Don't you think it is time to wash them?"

"No way! I might lose all my good luck." Tim pulled his pants back down over the socks and slipped his shoe back on. It was a few minutes before the smell got better.

"Bobby," said Mr. Reed as he looked at his notebook and then up at Bobby. "What do you find beautiful?"

Bobby stood up slowly. His eyes were still slightly red from the tears. He looked around the room cautiously. His voice seemed to hesitate, "I was lying in the middle of my grandfather's green pasture last summer." Bobby took a deep breath as he struggled for some confidence. "It was a hot day with a few rolling white clouds floating around in the sky. I felt the warmth of the ground against my back and the poking of the green grass through my shirt."

The teacher looked around the room at the students listening to Bobby's words. Every student was listening intently – except Maria! She was still looking at her dress - trying to remember what it looked like.

Bobby continued to talk – emphasizing each individual word, "My eyes looked upward between the floating white clouds into the dark blue of the sky. I wondered what it would be like to fly in a rocket through space. I saw a really strange looking cloud moving slowly above me. It seemed to be changing shape very quickly." Bobby's brown eyes looked down into the faces of the students for just a moment. "As it came closer, I could make out an eye in the cloud – then another eye. I watched a nose take shape between the two eyes." Bobby hesitated for a brief second. "Suddenly, I was staring at the face of a woman. The cloud looked like my mother!" Bobby's confidence continued to grow, as he watched the faces of the students and his teacher. "I could clearly see her eyes – and beautiful smiling mouth. She seemed to be looking down on me. I almost expected her to say something." Bobby looked down at his feet, and then back at his work. "In another second the cloud changed shape – and her face was gone. That moment was very beautiful."

The students stared at Bobby - even as he sat down. They had never heard a student describe such things in class. Some were wondering if his mother was alive. Others didn't know what to think.

Maria whispered to a girl by her. "I told you he was strange." Maria turned back to the teacher and raised her hand in the air. "Mr. Reed, I can describe my dress now!"

"Thank you, Maria," said Mr. Reed. "We'll try it again on another day."

Maria glanced toward Bobby. "I guess we have a new teacher's pet."

The girl beside Maria answered back, "Yeah, kind of cute too!"

"Yuk!" Maria made an ugly face to the girl. She looked at Bobby with a glance again.

"Thanks, Bobby." said Mr. Reed. "That was very good."

Tim poked Bobby in the back. "Where did all that come from? If I ever did that, my mom would faint right on the spot."

Bobby gave Tim a weak smile but said nothing. He tried not to look at the faces of the students still staring at him.

"Class. Take out your books and read the story beginning on page 121. We will talk about it in class tomorrow." Mr. Reed continued to think about what he had just heard from Bobby.

The students sneaked quick looks at Bobby every once in awhile, as they began to settle down to their assignments. They continued to think about the things they had just heard from the new kid. It wasn't long before everyone was reading quietly from their books.

The bell broke the silence of the room. The students gathered their things up and began leaving. Bobby waited until almost every student had left, then he worked his way toward the door.

Mr. Reed was sitting at his desk reading a student's paper — Bobby's paper. "Bobby." The teacher looked up. "Come here."

Bobby walked over to his desk shyly.

"I have been reading your homework. Did you have any help?" Mr. Reed stared at him.

"No sir." Bobby was very nervous. "I did it on my own."

The teacher smiled. "Your writing is very good. Who taught you to write like this?"

"My mom," answered Bobby. "I write stories all the time."

Mr. Reed looked at Bobby. "You tell her that she did a great job."

Bobby looked down at his feet shyly. "I will." He turned and walked quietly away from the teacher. Bobby stopped at the doorway, looked both ways down the hallway, and disappeared around the corner. He moved down the edge of the hallway cautiously - careful not to get in the way of any students. Several were telling their friends about Johnny and the new kid. They would stop talking as Bobby passed by. Once he was past them, they would say, "That's him. He's really going to get it!"

Bobby ignored the students and continued to look down at the floor as he walked. He tried not to be noticed.

Maria stood by Stephanie and Whitney. She saw Bobby coming toward her, "Better watch out! Johnny is going to get you!" She threw her hair back and laughed.

Bobby ignored her and continued to walk down the hallway. He looked up to see the sign in the hallway pointing to the principal's office as he walked under it. Bobby glanced into the principal's office as he passed by the door. Johnny was seated in an old wooden chair beside the secretary's desk. He was looking out the door right at Bobby.

Johnny's red and white splotches were starting to disappear. He looked into the wide brown eyes of Bobby. Johnny's face quickly turned to a vicious look. He was clearly thinking about revenge on the new kid.

Bobby looked away from Johnny quickly. "I wish Tim hadn't laughed at him – now he thinks it was me." Bobby looked nervously at the students passing by. He continued down the hallway to his next class.

CHAPTER 2

The Path of Life

The cafeteria was busy with students eating their lunches and visiting with their friends. Almost every table was full, when Johnny walked into the room. The students at tables talking and laughing a moment earlier - now whispered to each other. Most of them had heard about the trouble in Mr. Reed's classroom. The rumors were flowing fast and furious!

A girl whispered to a group of kids at a table, "I heard from a girl, who was in the office today - that Johnny was suspended from school." The girl made sure everyone was listening to her. "He hit Mr. Reed in class!" She leaned forward, "It was really ugly!"

"No he didn't!" said a boy in the group. "That's not what happened." He looked into the faces of the other students at the table. "Johnny got caught cheating in Mr. Reed's class!"

"How do you know?" said the girl in a huff.

"It was my paper that he used." Everyone in the group looked at the boy in horror. "I told Mr. Reed my paper had been stolen. I made an error on the second page of the test and accidentally tore the paper while I was erasing it. I guess Johnny just erased my name and turned it in. Mr. Reed saw the tear on the paper and knew it was my work." The boy leaned toward the center of the table. "Johnny didn't even know it was a different test in his class." The other students at the table laughed softly with the boy.

"It's you he must be looking for." said another boy. "He just walked in."

All eyes watched Johnny, as he walked into the room. Johnny's eyes searched everywhere looking for someone.

"You'd better get out of here!" said the girl in the group. "He must know it was you."

"It's okay. He doesn't know. His buddy over there at that table is the one who stole it and gave it to him." All eyes looked at Brad sitting with a couple of students near the door. "I wouldn't want to be him."

The group watched as Johnny walked over to the lunch line and stood at the end. His eyes continued to look around the room.

"Look at the anger on his face," said the girl. "Brad better get out of here in a hurry."

"Too late!" said the girl. "Johnny sees him."

The boys seated near Brad all began to pick up their things to leave.

"See ya later," said a boy beside Brad.

"Where are you going?" Brad's voice seemed to quiver. "You don't need to leave."

"I – uh – have to talk to my sister over there." The boy pointed to a group of girls sitting on the far side of the cafeteria. He picked up his tray and began walking toward them.

The remaining two boys at the table stood up as well. "We'd better go with him and make sure his sister doesn't beat him up." The boys gathered up their things and followed the boy.

"Thanks a lot." Brad watched as the three boys walked across the room to the group of girls. He could see the confusion on the sister's face as her brother sat down beside her. Brad watched as all eyes of the group turned to look at him. He looked back to the center of the room. Johnny was walking with his tray in hand toward him.

Johnny's eyes stared coldly at his friend, as he came closer. The red haired boy nodded his head slightly – Brad acknowledged the nod with a slight nod back.

Brad spoke softly in a whisper to himself, "Johnny doesn't look too mad. Maybe everything will be okay." He looked back down at his tray of food and took another bite of his peaches.

Johnny set his tray down beside Brad very slowly. He looked around the room to make sure no teachers were watching.

Brad looked forward just in time to see an elbow coming toward the side of his face, and turned sideways just enough to avoid the full impact of the blow. Brad felt his ear suddenly go numb and the pain that followed. "Ow!" He covered his ear with his hand. The ear became red almost immediately.

Johnny never looked once at Brad. Instead, he picked up his spoon and scooped a huge amount of mashed potatoes dripping in gravy into his mouth. His eyes looked around the room from table to table while Brad moaned softly. The students at other tables turned their eyes away when Johnny would look at them.

Brad wiped the tears away from his eyes with the sleeve of his shirt. "Why did you do that?"

"I got detention for a week," said Johnny. He scooped another large spoon full of potatoes in his mouth. Some of the gravy dripped down his chin onto the tray. "It was because of you that I got caught."

"How did I know it was a different test?" Brad removed his hand from the ear. The stinging was nearly gone. "I figured they were all the same."

"You figured wrong!" Johnny turned his head slowly toward Brad. His eyes sent a shiver up his back. "Was it the new kid or Tim that laughed, as I walked out of the room?"

"I – I'm not sure." Brad watched as the mean look spread across Johnny's face. "Uh – it was probably the new kid – I'm sure it was." Brad looked back down at the table to avoid the fiery eyes of Johnny. He felt a sense of relief that Johnny was now focused on the new kid. "Come to think about it – I'm sure it was him." Brad was beginning to believe that Johnny wouldn't hit him again. "I haven't seen the new kid since class ended. I wonder where he is?"

"He's right there." Johnny looked to the far corner of the cafeteria to a table next to the other door.

Brad looked across the room at the new kid sitting by himself. "He's a really strange kid. You should have heard his story in class."

Johnny elbowed Brad in the ribs. "I wonder why I didn't hear it."

Brad grimaced in pain for a second time. "I'm sorry." He rubbed his side with his hand. "It was my fault."

Johnny's angry eyes turned slowly toward Brad. He could clearly see the fear in Brad's eyes. "I want another milk! Get me a chocolate one."

Brad jumped up immediately from the table, walked up to the cook - handed her enough change to pay for additional milk, and returned with it to Johnny.

Johnny grunted, "Thanks." He took the milk quickly out of Brad's hands, tore it open, and guzzled it quickly down. Chocolate milk flowed from the corners of his mouth. Johnny wiped the milk off his face with the sleeves of his shirt, and then continued to stare at Bobby across the room.

Other students in the lunchroom were beginning to notice Johnny staring at the new kid. The loud voices in the room were slowly becoming a whisper.

Bobby sat next to the wall with his back to the door facing Johnny. His head was tilted downward as he ate. The brown curly hair covered his eyes which were not looking downward, but were actually watching Johnny and Brad very carefully. He had watched Johnny hit his blonde buddy two times. Bobby ate his lunch slowly – enjoying every bite of food as best he could.

A tray landed hard against the table right beside him. The food was an ugly mix of gravy, potatoes, and vegetables. Bobby flinched as he looked up into the smiling eyes of Tim. "Scared ya!" He stepped over the bench and sat down beside Bobby. "Bet you thought Johnny had you."

"Not really. He's over there staring at us." Bobby looked back across the room at Johnny.

Tim's eyes turned slowly until he saw the glare of Johnny. "Oops! I thought he was sent home." Tim got back up from the bench. "Looks like a good time for me to disappear." He walked to the far side of the cafeteria away from Johnny and Brad, placed his tray in the cleanup window, and walked out the door. Tim stopped to look back through the glass window. Johnny was still glaring at the new kid. Tim took a deep breath and disappeared.

Bobby continued to eat his lunch slowly. He kept watching Johnny across the room through his hair. Bobby's heart began to pound, as he watched Johnny pick up his tray, and start across the room to him. Most of the students in the cafeteria quit talking, as they watched the red haired bully walking toward Bobby.

Johnny began to smile in his mean way as he came closer. His freckles appeared twice as red. His blue eyes seemed to squint, as he stared at Bobby. Brad was following right behind him.

Bobby continued to eat as the two boys set their trays down straight across from him. He tried to avoid looking directly into their faces, and felt fear swelling in his chest.

"Brad, I think something stinks at this table." Johnny kept staring at Bobby.

"I don't smell anything," Brad said. He looked at Johnny's face, and then realized what he meant.

"Yeah! It really stinks here - really bad." Brad turned toward Bobby. "What do you think it is?"

"It smells like a chicken. We must have a chicken over here." Johnny stared at Bobby without blinking his eyes.

Bobby cringed as he felt a hand touch his shoulder. He looked up to see the smiling face of Mr. Roberts. "Bobby... isn't it?"

"Yes sir." Bobby answered quietly.

"How's your day going?" asked Mr. Roberts. He looked across the table at the other two boys - looking down at their trays - trying to ignore him.

Bobby hesitated. "It's going fine Mr. Roberts."

The teacher looked over the situation. His eyes looked hard at Johnny and Brad. "Don't mind me boys. I'm just going to stand here and make sure no one is getting into any trouble."

Johnny could see his fun was over. He nodded his head backward for Brad to follow. Johnny looked directly into Bobby's eyes. "See you later." It was definitely a warning of things to come. "Have a great day!"

Bobby watched Johnny and Brad place their trays in the clean up window. They moved toward the door with Mr. Roberts right behind them.

"That was close!" Tim jumped into the air and landed right next to Bobby.

"Where did you disappear to?" asked Bobby.

"I was watching to see if you needed any help." stated Tim.

Bobby thought for a moment. "Did you go get Mr. Roberts?"

Tim stood up, "Maybe." He laughed a couple of times. "See ya later."

Bobby watched Tim as he walked through the cafeteria. He seemed fascinated by this mess of a kid. Bobby returned to eating his lunch in quiet. Most of the students had left the cafeteria by now.

The cooks were beginning to clean the tables and put things away. They smiled at Bobby and left him alone.

Bobby had eaten about as slow as he could. There was nothing left on the tray to eat. He picked up his empty tray and walked across the room. Bobby placed the tray on a stack in the window.

A cook rinsing off dirty trays, looked at Bobby's tray and then at him. She saw the tray was absolutely clean of all food and smiled, "We have some ice cream bars that will melt if some one doesn't eat them. Do you have enough room for one or two?"

A smile came across his face. "I sure do." Bobby hadn't eaten ice cream in long time.

"Come over to the door. I'll get them." The cook disappeared to the back of the kitchen, and then returned to the counter. She handed Bobby two ice cream bars. "Sure glad we found someone to eat these. It would have been a waste."

Bobby sat down at a table near by and ate the first bar quickly. He sighed deeply, and then took his time with second one – enjoying every bite. The last time he had ice cream was during the summer at his grandparents' home.

"Thank you." Bobby smiled as he walked toward the door of the cafeteria.

"You are welcome." The cook returned a big smile. She watched Bobby until he walked through the cafeteria doors. She thought to herself, "Good kid."

Bobby stopped outside the door – looked both directions down the hallway. He thought about hiding in the bathroom, but quickly remembered what had happened before school. Bobby needed a safe place to go until classes started. He looked cautiously back down the hallways again. There were a few kids standing around, but none of them was a tall red haired boy with huge freckles and vicious blue eyes. Bobby took a deep breath and began to head toward the library – a safe place to hang out for awhile.

The library was full of students. Most were trying to find a warm place, instead of standing around outside. Bobby stood at the doorway for a second, searching the room for Johnny and Brad. They were no where to be found. He relaxed a little and entered the room.

Bobby took the books from his backpack and placed them in the check-in slot on the side of the counter. He made sure his grandmother's book was not in the group, walked back to the science section, and picked up a book about dinosaurs - similar to the one he checked in. Bobby stepped around the end of the bookshelf and jumped back. On the carpet in front of him was Tim lying on his side. His body was frozen as if he were dead. Bobby stared closely to see if Tim was breathing. He noticed a tiny smile beginning to form near the corners of Tim's mouth. Bobby wondered what this strange kid was up to.

"Do you know what I am?" Tim remained frozen, but spoke to Bobby out the corner of his mouth. "A dinosaur... an extinct dinosaur!"

Bobby couldn't believe that Tim would do such a thing. He actually looked like the shape of a dinosaur skeleton on the ground – a messy dinosaur! Bobby broke out into laughter. He laughed so hard that tears streamed down his cheeks. Other students heard the laughter and came over to the bookshelf to see what was so funny. Bobby told them there was an extinct dinosaur on the floor. They too began to laugh loudly as they saw Tim.

Mrs. Wilson, the librarian, came over to see what the laughter was about. "That's enough!" She looked down at Tim on the floor. "Timothy!"

Tim got up to his feet. "Time to become even more extinct!" He gave Bobby a big grin and left the room.

Mrs. Wilson smiled as she watched Tim leave the library.

Bobby continued to laugh softly. He wondered what this messy kid's next antic would be.

"I see you like dinosaur books." Mrs. Wilson was standing beside Bobby. "Here's another book you may be interested in." She handed a book to Bobby. "It's about digging up the skeletons of dinosaurs and figuring out what they looked like back then."

"Thanks." Bobby took the book and went over to a table to sit down. He placed his things down beside him and began to look at the dinosaur book. Bobby kept the book in front of his face.

"Tim's pretty funny," said a girl's voice.

Bobby looked over the top of the book into the dark eyes of a girl. Her long brown hair hung neatly down over her shoulders. Her clothes were stylish. Everything about her seemed just right.

"I'm Liz – Tim's sister." She continued to smile at Bobby. "We're twins."

Bobby seemed to stare at Liz for the longest time. He couldn't imagine how Tim could be such a mess and his sister so... perfect. He answered with caution, "Hi."

"Do you have a name?" She seemed to have some of Tim's attitude.

"Bobby." He watched her carefully to see if she was going to say or do something mean. He wondered if she was one of the gossiping trio's friends.

"You're new here – aren't you?" Liz placed her books on the table and stared deeply into his eyes.

Bobby could see that she wasn't going to be ignored. "I moved here a few days ago."

"Where were you from?" she asked quickly.

"We lived in a small town across the state." Bobby was careful what he told her. He was becoming suspicious.

"Why did you move here?" Liz watched Bobby's face change color. She knew it was the wrong question.

Bobby watched her face for a moment without answering. He wondered what she was up to. Was she just another student being mean or was she just curious? Bobby stacked his books in a pile and stood up. "I've got to check out these books. It was nice to meet you."

Liz stared in disbelief. She couldn't believe that Bobby had just walked away from her.

Tim appeared again from no where and sat down beside his twin sister. The two of them watched Bobby walk across the library to the check out counter. "What do you think? He seems nice enough." said Tim.

"What do I think? I think you deserve this." Liz stepped on her brother's foot. "You asked me to be nice to him – and he just walked away from me."

"What did you do?" answered Tim. "Did you say something mean?"

"Me!" Liz moved toward Tim's face until her nose nearly touched his nose. She was looking deep into his eyes at close range. "You want to repeat that again?" Liz's eyes grew larger and larger.

Tim could see he was probably going to get hurt again. "I'm sorry. I guess it was entirely my fault!"

"You guess?" Liz backed up a step. "It was your bad idea for me to be nice to him." Then she stepped on his foot again.

"Ouch!" Tim rubbed his foot. Things were not going as he had planned.

"It was not just a bad idea – it was a typical Tim idea!" Liz stood up and looked down at her brother. "Need I say more?" She turned away and walked out the door.

Mrs. Wilson was checking out books as fast as she could before the bell would ring. Bobby stood in front of the counter waiting for his turn. He was the last person in the line. Bobby finally got his turn. "Do you have a Robert Frost book of poetry?"

Mrs. Wilson stopped for a second and looked at Bobby. "Excuse me. I don't think I heard you right. What did you say?"

Bobby repeated the question. "Do you have a Robert Frost book of poetry?"

"Sure." She seemed a little stunned by the question.

Mrs. Wilson looked around the library to see if there were anymore students to check out. She saw no one. "Come on. Let's see what we have on the shelf." Mrs. Wilson walked Bobby over to a shelf in the corner of the room. "There should be two books on the shelf. I don't think kids ever read them."

The librarian began to scan the shelf with her eyes first. Then, her hand moved slowly over the top of several books one at a time. Her fingers came to a stop over a small old book. Mrs. Wilson removed the book and handed it to Bobby. "Wait. Here's another one." She handed the second book to Bobby as well.

"Thank you," said Bobby politely.

"You're welcome." She watched Bobby carefully. "Have you read poetry by Robert Frost before?"

"No," answered Bobby. "My mother used to read it to me at night before I went to sleep. Sometimes, she would tell me what the poem meant – sometimes I figured it out."

"That must have been fun," returned the librarian. "Do you remember any of the poems?"

"Some of them." Bobby closed his eyes slowly and began to repeat a poem. His voice was clear and easily understood - his emotions could be felt in the words he spoke.

Mrs. Wilson watched Bobby in awe. "What does that poem mean?"

"It is about life." Bobby seemed to reach deep inside his brain. "Our lives are about paths. When the path comes to a fork and divides into two, we must decide whether to go right – go left – or return to where we started. Sometimes we must go down a path that no one has traveled before. It's those choices in life that we must make - and to do so without regret of what might have been."

The librarian was hypnotized by Bobby's words. "What you have said is wonderful!"

Bobby spoke modestly, "Not me – it was Robert Frost." He smiled at Mrs. Wilson, "...and my mom!"

"You are very right, but I don't think I have ever heard it said quite like that," said Mrs. Wilson. "Your mother can be very proud of you."

Bobby's smile changed to a serious look. "Thank you. I must get to class." Bobby walked over to the counter and checked the book out with the librarian.

Mrs. Wilson watched Bobby, as he left the library. She repeated to herself what Bobby had said, "The paths of life. No regrets," said the librarian quietly, as she went back to shelving books. She wondered what had changed his smile so quickly.

Bobby walked into the hallway from the library, looking at a clock on the wall straight across from him. He needed to hurry to Mr. Robert's science class. Bobby turned to the left and walked quickly along the side of the hallway. There were very few students left in the hallway. His walk changed to a run, as he thought, "I don't want to be late!"

Mr. Roberts was standing at the doorway watching Bobby running down the hall toward him. "Good afternoon!"

Bobby looked up into the warm friendly face of the science teacher. "Good afternoon." Bobby smiled back in return.

His eyes looked past the teacher into the classroom. There were many round tables scattered around the room with four students seated at each one. Bobby could see that all the tables had four students except for one table near the door beside a giant cage.

"Let's get you a seat." The teacher closed the door and walked Bobby toward the only empty seat in the room. The students were busy visiting each other and doing things – no one seemed to notice Bobby.

He quickly recognized one of the students seated next to the empty chair. It was Tim's twin sister, Liz. She looked up and smiled at Bobby as he sat down.

Mr. Roberts placed his hand on Bobby's shoulder, smiled again, and walked toward the center of the classroom. He stopped to talk with a couple of students at different tables along the way.

Bobby watched the teacher as he moved around the room. Mr. Roberts seemed like a kind person genuinely interested in kids. Bobby took his backpack off and placed it on the floor beside the chair.

Bobby's eyes turned to a boy seated on his other side. He had never seen him before.

The eyes of the boy looked up. "Hi! I'm Jamal."

"I'm Bobby."

A girl sitting straight across from Bobby sat looking down at something in her lap. She seemed familiar. Her long brown hair covered her face. The girl looked up quickly when she heard Bobby's voice. Their eyes met each other at the same moment. It was Stephanie!

Bobby's mind quickly went back to the meanness of the three girls at the beginning of the day. His voice seemed to escape his mouth, "Great! Now I have another one of the 'Trio of Terror' to contend with."

Liz and Jamal both heard the comment and broke into immediate laughter. Students in the area turned to see what was so funny.

Stephanie instantly opened her mouth but no sound came out. She just sat there staring at Bobby, trying to think of something to say back.

Bobby leaned back in his chair against the cage behind him. He thought, "That was a really a stupid thing to do – but kind of funny." He placed his hands behind his head, looked up at the ceiling to avoid Stephanie's angry face.

At that very instant a loud roaring hissing sound came from the cage directly behind Bobby's hands and head. It was so loud that every student in the room and Mr. Roberts looked in Bobby's direction. Bobby figured a large dinosaur or some horrible creature was about to eat him. He tried to jump out of the chair, but fell onto the floor. His whole body seemed to be frozen in fear.

The entire room was silent, and then a roar of laughter began – including Mr. Roberts.

"Bobby," shouted Roberts between his laughs. "I'd like to introduce you to Herman – our class alligator."

Bobby crawled on the floor closer to the cage and peeked inside. Sure enough, there was a huge alligator in the cage. Herman must have been close to five feet in length! His eyes remained unblinking - just staring at Bobby. He seemed to be saying, "Gotcha!"

The laughter in the classroom finally died down as Bobby stood up and slipped back into his chair. Liz and Jamal continued to giggle as Bobby looked at each of them – even Stephanie was smiling. Bobby finally smiled back, "Good impression on the first day!"

Stephanie nodded her head, "Yep!"

Mr. Roberts was trying not to laugh anymore, as he wiped away a tear or two from his eyes. "Today, we are going to begin studying a distant cousin of Herman – the frog!" The teacher moved to the front of the classroom and pulled down a chart on the wall. It was a giant picture of a frog. "Who can tell me something about a frog?"

A girl near the front of the room raised her hand. "They give you warts!"

"No they don't," said a boy in her group. "Only toads can do that."

Jamal raised his hand. "Actually, you are both wrong."

Liz whispered in Bobby's ear, "Watch this. Jamal is a walking genus."

"The frog is a tailless amphibian with a smooth skin and two large hind legs designed for jumping. True frogs belong to the scientific family of Ranidae." Jamal sat back in his chair looking at the class. "And toads do not create warts. Warts are caused by a virus."

"See what I mean," said Liz quietly to Bobby.

Bobby looked at Liz and nodded his head in agreement.

"Thanks Jamal," said the teacher. "Anyone else have something to add?" Mr. Roberts waited, but no one raised his or her hand to speak. "Good. Each of you will work as a group to find similarities and differences between Herman and a frog. You have fifteen minutes to work as a group."

Liz, Stephanie, Jamal, and Bobby looked at each other for a minute without talking. Finally, Liz broke the silence, "They're both green."

"They both have two eyes," stated Stephanie.

Jamal seemed annoyed by Stephanie's answer of the obvious. "Both of them have legs specialized for their environment. The frog has legs adapted for jumping, and the alligator has legs adapted for swimming and crawling." Jamal's vast knowledge was apparent every time he talked.

"The frog is an amphibian, and the alligator is a reptile." said Bobby in a voice lacking confidence. "Both lay eggs - both are cold-blooded."

Jamal and the girls looked at Bobby in surprise.

"The alligator eggs are hatched on the beach in the warm sand. The babies crawl into the water as soon as the hatch." Bobby's confidence began to grow. "Frogs lay their eggs in the water. Newly born frogs breathe under water through gills. The gills disappear and lungs form as the frog gets older."

Jamal placed his hand up flat in the air beside Bobby to get a 'high five'. The two boys slapped hands.

Bobby looked toward Liz. Her hand was up in the air as well – the two slapped hands and smiled. Bobby looked across the table at Stephanie. She didn't have her hand up in the air, but was staring at Bobby with a look of question on her face.

"One difference between Herman and a frog," said Liz in a giggle. "Herman can really scare a person with that sound he makes." Her eyes twinkled as she looked at Bobby.

"Tell me about it!" Bobby smiled at each person in the group – including Stephanie. Stephanie smiled back. This was something unexpected.

Mr. Roberts asked each group to explain their similarities and differences. Jamal spoke for their group in his genus way. As usual, everyone was impressed with his great knowledge, but was surprised when he told them the information was from Bobby. All of the eyes in the room stared at him.

"In front of you is a metal pan with a sealed lid on top." Mr. Roberts watched as the students began to reach for the metal pans. "There are switches on each side of the pan, which keeps the lids down tight and sealed. Turn the switches sideways and take the lid off."

The students turned the switches sideways and removed the airtight lids. The first whiff of the smell hit each student immediately. It was the smell of chemicals to preserve the frog lying in the center of the pan. Some students were gagging from the smell. The sight of a preserved frog lying on its back shocked others.

Bobby looked across at Stephanie. She had her hand over her mouth. Her skin was changing to a pale white. "I think... I think... I'm going to...' She placed both hands over her mouth and ran out of the room. Mr. Roberts followed right behind her.

Liz looked at Bobby. "I think she was about to say - puke!" Liz did a small shiver over her entire body, and looked back down at her frog.

"Look at the side of the head," said Jamal, unfazed by Stephanie's sickness as he pointed to a small round area. "That's the ear."

Liz searched her frog for the ear. "Where are you little ear?" She smiled at Bobby and Jamal. "There you are!" She pointed to the tiny ear with her pencil. There were definitely similarities between Tim and Liz.

Bobby placed the frog on the palm of his hand and looked at it carefully. He held it as if it were a puppet and spoke for it, "My name is Freddy Frog." Bobby tried to imitate the sounds of a frog as he spoke. "Once I lived in a giant pond near the river." He sighed deeply. "I ate flies and mosquitoes every day." Bobby stuck out his tongue like he was catching insects, and then chewed them up. "Ummmmmm good!" Bobby's real personality was beginning to show. "I asked the beautiful princess to kiss me, and change me into a handsome prince again, but instead she pickled me in this pan."

Jamal and Liz both laughed at Bobby's 'frog show'. They were quite surprised by the new kid's sense of humor.

Mr. Roberts walked Stephanie back into the room to her seat. He placed the lid back down on her frog. Stephanie still looked a little pale. She saw the frog in Bobby's hand and looked away.

Bobby closed his fingers around the frog. He glanced at Liz and Jamal still smiling about his frog routine.

Mr. Roberts stood at the front of the classroom. "I'd like everyone to place your frogs back in the pans and seal the lids. You will all need to wash your hands." He walked table to table making sure the students were following his directions.

Bobby could see that Stephanie's color had returned to her skin. He took her pan and tightened the lid down for her. The look on Stephanie's face was a definite 'thank you'.

"Tomorrow," said Mr. Roberts in a loud voice to all the students. "We will begin dissecting your frogs." He smiled, as it was exciting for some students, while others were already feeling sick.

Liz turned toward Bobby. She could see he was looking at the clock. His face was no longer happy for some reason. "Class was great today!"

Bobby looked back at Liz, "Yep!" He tried to force a smile.

"See you tomorrow," said Liz as the bell rang. She grabbed her things and headed out the door quickly.

Bobby picked his things up and walked out of the classroom behind her. He was unaware that Mr. Roberts was watching him leave.

"I'm glad that is the last class of the day." Jamal was walking beside him.

"Me too!" Bobby felt a little relief knowing someone was walking with him. His mind went back to the start of the day in Mr. Reed's classroom. He wondered if Johnny and Brad were waiting for him somewhere ahead.

"That was pretty funny when Stephanie got sick!" Jamal laughed a little, as he walked. "Stephanie, Maria, and Whitney really are the 'Trio of Terror'."

"Trio of Terror," Bobby thought to himself. Now he wasn't really as sure if Stephanie was as mean as the other two.

"I've got to get home." Jamal turned down a side hallway and disappeared in the sea of students. "See you tomorrow."

Bobby saw Mr. Reed's classroom just ahead. He looked into the room. Mr. Reed was sitting at his desk. Directly in front of him were Johnny and Brad.

Johnny looked up at Bobby. He mouthed the words, "I will get you!"

Bobby moved quickly by the doorway and down the hallway to the giant front doors. He looked outside at the gray clouds floating above – these were definitely snow clouds. Bobby pulled his worn out coat out of his backpack and slipped it on quickly. He zipped it up tight, and stepped outside into the cold air.

"Home is ten blocks away," thought Bobby, as he walked slowly down the stairs. "I will be home in about twenty minutes. At least, I know where the bully and his buddy are at this very moment."

"Hey there!" Tim ran up to Bobby. "Which way are you heading?"

"That way." Bobby pointed toward his house.

"I live in that direction also." said Tim. "Usually I have to walk with Liz, but tonight she went over to a friend's house."

The two boys talked about Johnny and Brad as they walked. Bobby told Tim about science class, Stephanie getting sick, and Herman! Tim laughed loudly, and asked Bobby to tell him the story again about the alligator. It felt good for Bobby to have someone to share the story with.

Tim stopped, "This is my house. See you tomorrow." Tim ran up the stairs and into the house.

Bobby wasn't surprised. There were two bicycles in the driveway. One bicycle was standing neatly by the back door; the other was lying on its side in the middle of the driveway. There was no doubt in his mind, which bicycle belonged to Liz, and which one belonged to Tim.

Bobby glanced around him in all directions. He was alone again. Bobby hurried the rest of the way home.

CHAPTER 3

Tomatoes Ala Yuk

Bobby walked several more blocks down the street, until he came to an old house surrounded by a broken down picket fence needing a new paint job and lots of repairs. The gate didn't swing open, as one of the hinges was broken. Bobby picked up the gate gently, opened it, stepped inside, and closed it carefully so as not to cause anymore damage.

He stood in front of the old house for a moment staring at its windows covered in clear plastic to help keep the cold out. It was not a pretty sight to look at. The house needed to be painted like the fence. The bushes around the house were large and untrimmed, looking like hundreds of bony fingers reaching out in all directions. He reminded himself that this was not his home – it was just a place to live!

Bobby closed his eyes - trying to remember each detail of his real home so far away. It was a small white house surrounded by a white picket fence, which Bobby had helped paint with his mother on a warm day last spring. Colorful flowers were planted along the sides of the fence and down the concrete walkway to the front door.

He could picture in his mind the dark green grass of the yard surrounding the house. Two large trees stood in the center of the yard, which he had climbed many times. Bobby's heart began to ache, as he remembered his beautiful home so far away. His dark eyes opened slowly - looking at the ugliness in front of him. "This will never be my home!"

The boy sighed deeply, reached out for the worn doorknob, and entered the front door. Bobby shouted halfheartedly, "I'm home Mom!" He set his things down on an old chair by the front door, took his coat off, and hung it on a hook. The air in the house was cool, as it was hard to keep the house warm with all the cracks around the doors and windows. Extra heat cost lots of money – something they didn't have. He would go downstairs to his bedroom in a little while for his sweatshirt to help keep him warm.

"Bobby, I'm in the kitchen." A woman's voice shouted from the back of the house. "I'm getting ready to fix something special for dinner tonight!"

Bobby looked around the room at the few pieces of furniture here and there. All of their furniture was old and nearly worn out. Most of it had been bought at a used furniture store nearby. His favorite was an old tan couch facing the television on the far side of the room. The springs in the seat of the couch were so bad, that Bobby would go straight up into the air when his dad sat down on the other end.

Once in awhile Bobby and his parents would treat themselves to popcorn and hot tea while watching television from the old couch. Sugar for the tea made it even more special. They didn't have cable or satellite television, and were lucky if they could get two channels off the old broken antennae on the ceiling of the house.

Bobby remembered the living room of his old house back home. It was far different from this one. There were no cracks around the doors and windows - the house was always warm. His mother kept the house freshly painted and always clean. A decent couch sat against one wall facing a new television on the opposite wall. The other wall had a small table by a rocking chair. On the floor was a basket of yarn. Each night Bobby's mother would work on knitting a blanket or something for an hour or two before going to bed. It was her way of ending a perfect day.

Bobby remembered a tall polished wooden piano, which stood against the remaining wall with framed pictures of the family sitting on its top. Bobby's mother wanted him to play the piano, but he wanted to play the drums. They would argue back and forth on which one it would be. Unfortunately, he never had a chance do either. The piano and most of the furniture had to be sold when they moved.

He walked across the spotless old wooden floor of the living room to the kitchen. The old floor squeaked with each step that he took. Bobby was beginning to get used to the sound. Downstairs in his bedroom - it was even worse.

"Hi sweetie!" Bobby's mother was standing at the sink with her back to him. "How was school today? Did you make any new friends?"

"It was okay." Bobby decided to not say anything about the red hair boy and his buddy. "I met a couple of new kids today and had my first science class."

His mother turned around to face him. She had the same dark brown eyes and hair as Bobby. Her warm smile seemed to fill the coolness of the house with warmth. "Tell me all about your day." She sat down at a small table in the kitchen with three wooden chairs around it, and motioned Bobby to sit across from her.

Bobby told her everything about his day except the part with the bullies. He knew it would upset her - there was no reason for that. Some things were better left unsaid. They both laughed hard, when Bobby told her about the alligator scaring him to death and Tim acting like an extinct dinosaur in the library.

"Did you check out some new books?" His mother's beautiful brown eyes twinkled like the stars in the sky. "What are we going to read tonight?"

"I have a great book on dinosaurs and..." Bobby was interrupted by her.

"You and those dinosaurs," His mother giggled. "The next thing you know - you will want to be an archeologist."

"No, Mom," said Bobby. He seemed to sit up a little taller in the chair. "I want to be a teacher or a writer some day." His dark eyes stared straight into the face of his mother. She could see the seriousness and determination of his words.

She smiled softly, "I think that would be great."

His mother reached out to his curly brown hair and patted him gently on the head. "I'm proud of you." She played with one of his curls for a moment - knowing that it aggravated him. "What was the other book you checked out?"

"Something for you!" Bobby watched his mother's eyes twinkle.

"Did you find another book on Robert Frost?" His mother waited for the answer.

"Yes," said Bobby. "Mrs. Wilson, our librarian, helped me find it. Actually, she found two books."

"How about we read a couple of poems together after dinner?" asked his mother.

"I'd like that," answered Bobby. Reading together with his mother was one of his favorite times each day.

Bobby's mother continued to look at her son with pride – it was so easy to see that he loved to learn. She was determined Bobby would have a good education, and hopefully go to college one day. It would be hard, but she would make sure her son got there. She thought, "I was the first person in my family to graduate from high school – Bobby will be the first to go to college!"

"What are you thinking about?" Bobby could tell his mother was in deep thought.

"Just how proud I am of you." answered his mother. "I am so very proud of you."

"I know you are," answered Bobby. Reluctantly, he asked, "What's for dinner?" Bobby knew it would be one of three choices - boiled potatoes and green beans, or stewed tomatoes and macaroni, or stewed tomatoes in dried pieces of bread. Once in awhile they would have a small piece of meat with their dinner, but he was pretty sure that wouldn't be today.

"We are having Tomatoes Ala Bread!" His mother watched Bobby's reaction. It wasn't much of a meal, but it would feed the three of them.

"Great!" answered Bobby. "I'm starved!" He thought, "They should have called it Tomatoes Ala Yuk!"

It wasn't a difficult meal to make. His mother took a quart of canned stewed tomatoes and poured them into a large pot on the stove. She would boil the tomatoes, mix in dried breadcrumbs, and turn the heat on the stove down to a low temperature. Last, she would season the 'Yuk' with salt and pepper, and let it cook for about ten minutes. The cooked mixture was pretty ugly to look at, but the 'Yuk' did fill a hungry stomach.

"I will fix dinner in about an hour," said his mother. "Your father should be home about then." She hesitated for a moment. "He has to work tonight on his extra job for a few hours."

Bobby disliked not seeing his father very much. He would get to see his father in the morning for a few minutes, just before he left for his day job; then he would see him again for a little bit at dinner before he left for his night job.

"Dad will be home for only an hour or so." The smile on his mother's face quickly disappeared.

"Does he get enough sleep?" Bobby already knew the answer to the question. "How does he do it?"

Bobby's mother ignored the question. Bobby knew it was best to drop the conversation.

His mother pushed back her chair, stood up, and returned to the sink. "Grandpa sent some fresh apples today from back home. I'm going to make an apple cobbler for dessert."

"Apple cobbler!" Bobby's eyes lit up. This would get his mind off of his father and how hard he was working. "We haven't had apple cobbler in a long time! Can I help?"

Bobby's mother looked down at her son. "Sure. I just washed the apples – you can peel them."

Bobby walked over to the sink and looked down. He could see ten or twelve brightly colored red apples in the bottom of the sink. Bobby would have liked to grab one right then and ate it, but he knew there would be no extras for that sort of thing. He picked up the knife on the counter and eagerly waited to start.

His mother placed three large bowls in front of them on the counter. The two stood at the sink side by side. Bobby peeled each apple carefully, so as not to waste any of the fruit. He handed the peeled apple to his mother, placed his peelings in the first bowl, and selected a new apple from the sink to do it all over again.

Bobby's mother took the peeled apple and carefully cut the apple in four pieces. She took each piece of the divided apple and cut away the core and seeds, and placed them into the second bowl. Lastly, his mother took the clean pieces of the apple, rinsed them with water, and cut them into small chunks in the third bowl.

"Let's have some music." Bobby's mother walked across the kitchen to an old radio on top of the refrigerator and turned it on. With a big smile on her face she went back to cutting up apples.

It didn't take long for Bobby and his mother to cut up the apples. The first bowl was filled with apple peelings to the top of the rim. Some people would have thrown them away in the garbage, but not Bobby's mother. She would turn those peels into jelly late tonight or tomorrow. The second bowl with apple cores and seeds would be cooked, and made into a small bowl of applesauce. Nothing would be wasted!

"Oh by the way!" said his mom casually. "Your grandpa left you something." Bobby's mom opened a cabinet door above the counter slowly and reached inside. She pulled back a beautiful golden yellow apple. "He brought this just for you."

Bobby stared at the apple, as his mother placed it in his hand. "T- t – thanks." He never knew an apple could be so special.

"Go do your homework before Dad gets home," said his mother warmly. "I will start dinner after I finish making the cobbler." She watched Bobby walk to the front door, get his books, and walk through a doorway that led downstairs to the basement where his bedroom was. Her eyes turned back to the counter and the three bowls, as she wondered how they were going to continue stretching food. There just wasn't enough money for everything. Small tears swelled up in her dark brown eyes as she stared at the three bowls. She placed her hands on the counter and looked down at her feet. Tiny tears fell to the floor below her like the first droplets of rain in a spring storm.

Bobby's mother couldn't help remembering her small beautiful house back home that was lost when the factory was closed. Everyone lost their jobs including Bobby's father and her. They sold everything and moved to the city in hopes of a new beginning. She watched as tear drops continued to fall to the floor below. Bobby's mother stood motionless for a moment looking down at the puddles of tears below. She sighed deeply. It was a hard time, but they would survive. Bobby's mother picked up a towel, wiped the tears from her eyes, and started to fix the rest of the cobbler.

Bobby turned on the basement stairway light and walked carefully down each creaking step. It was warmer in the basement than in the house above. He figured it was because of the old furnace in the corner of the room. Bobby stepped down the last step onto the concrete floor covered by an old worn carpet that Bobby's dad had scrounged somewhere.

His bed was placed in the far corner of the room with a small round table and a wooden chair beside it. Bobby laid his books and the apple gently on the table, and then sat down in the chair. He placed all his things neatly on the tabletop, and turned on a lamp hanging down from the roof above. Bobby stared at the apple for a few minutes – it looked so good. He would save it for later.

The smells of apple cobbler cooking in the stove began to spread throughout the entire house. Bobby's mother looked up at the clock. She knew her husband would be home in a few minutes to eat a quick dinner and leave again for his second job. It would take only a few minutes to make 'Tomatoes Ala Bread'. She thought, "This should have been called 'Tomatoes Ala Yuk." - never knowing that this was her son's exact words. She turned to a noise in the living room.

Bobby's father walked into the front door at that moment. He was nothing like Bobby or his mother. His hair was red, which made his bright blue eyes stand out against his white freckled skin. He wasn't tall, but he wasn't short either.

His dad took off his worn out coat and placed it besides Bobby's coat. He looked at Bobby's coat carefully and shook his head slightly back and forth. "Bobby has to have a coat better than this!" His father turned and walked slowly toward the kitchen. The smell of apple cobbler seemed to hit his nose all at once. A slight smile crept across his face. "What smells so good?"

Bobby's mother walked across the kitchen and gave him a big kiss. "My dad sent us a few apples today."

He looked at the cobbler cooling on the counter, and then lifted the lid on the pot. His blue eyes gazed down into the pot of 'Yuk'. He knew his wife was watching his reaction. "Umm, smells good. How long before we eat?"

"About five or ten minutes," said Bobby's mother. "Why don't you rest for a little bit?"

"Sounds good. I'll go in the living room and lay down for a few minutes." Bobby's father walked slowly back into the living room, and sat down on the old couch, turned sideways, and stretched out from one end to the other. It was only a few seconds and he was fast asleep.

Bobby's mother watched her husband for a few moments. She didn't know how long her husband could keep up this pace – he was totally exhausted! She suddenly realized that Bobby was standing beside her. Bobby's mother placed an arm around her son as they both watched his father sleep. Soon, Bobby's father began snoring loudly. Bobby and his mother looked at each other with grins on their faces, and walked back into the kitchen.

A short time later, Bobby gently shook his father. "Dad." Bobby shook him some more. "It's time to wake up."

The snoring stopped, as two blue eyes slowly opened to look at Bobby. A slight smile formed on his dad's face. He grabbed Bobby quickly and began to tickle him. Bobby was extremely ticklish. His giggles soon turned to loud laughter, as he tickled Bobby everywhere.

Bobby's mother stood in the kitchen doorway laughing at the two playing. "Dinner's on the table."

Bobby grabbed his father's hand and pulled him up from the couch. The two walked into the kitchen and sat down at the old table. In the center of the table was a steaming bowl of 'Tomatoes Ala Yuk'.

"I made ice tea for dinner." said Bobby's mother proudly. "Would either of you like some?"

"I'll have some of that good stuff!" said Bobby's father. "Tea sounds great!"

"Me too!" said Bobby. Hot tea – ice tea – it was all the same to him; he loved to drink tea any time.

She placed ice in each glass and filled them to the brim with tea from the refrigerator. Bobby's mother smiled as she watched her two guys drink from the glasses.

"That's great mom!" said Bobby. "You sweetened it just right."

"It's perfect," said his father, as he took a long drink. "How about a refill?" He smiled with a large grin, as he watched his wife reach for the pitcher of tea.

"No problem." Bobby's mother refilled everyone's glasses. "You can have as much as you want."

All three of them set down to a bowl of 'Yuk' and ice tea. Bobby's mother didn't look up for several minutes.

"The tomatoes are..." Bobby spoke with a hesitation. "They're great!"

Bobby's parents sat for a moment in silence, thinking about what Bobby had just said.

His mother broke into loud laughter. "This isn't 'Tomatoes Ala Bread' –it's Tomato Ala ..."

"Yuk?" Bobby added softly.

She stopped laughing for a moment and looked at Bobby. It was exactly the word Bobby's mother was thinking of. "From now on this will be called 'Tomatoes Ala Yuk'!" His mother laughed even harder.

Bobby and his father sat quietly for a moment watching her, and then they began to laugh with her. Soon, all three of them began to eat their bowls of 'Yuk'.

"How was your day son?" asked Bobby's father, as he ate each bite of 'Yuk' slowly.

It was a normal thing at dinner for each member of the family to tell about things that happened in their day. Bobby skipped all the parts about the bullies.

His father really enjoyed the part about the alligator. He sat back in his chair and laughed hard.

Bobby's mom smiled when it came to her turn. "I'm going to let my work talk for me today." She reached inside her pockets and pulled out two rolled up red things made from yarn. "Bobby. These are for you."

Bobby took the two objects and unrolled them. The two objects were a pair of slippers knitted by his mother to help keep his feet warm on the cold floors. Very quickly, he took off his old shoes and slipped the new slippers on his feet. He stood up and walked over to the sink and back. "They're warm and soft," said Bobby, as he looked down at his feet. "Thanks Mom."

His mother sat in her chair with a big grin on her face. She had worked all day knitting them from left over yarn. Bobby's mother turned to her husband, "And something special for you." She stood up and walked over to the stove, opened the door, and reached into the stove for a large pan with two kitchen towels. The heat of the stove escaped through the opened door. The smell of cinnamon and apples was even stronger. She turned around with a dish in her hands. "Apple cobbler!"

"Wow!" Bobby's father looked at the apple cobbler - his blue eyes shining. "Let's have some right now - while it is still warm."

"Hand me your plates." Bobby's mother served each of them a large scoop of apple cobbler on their plates. She watched as her guys began to eat the crispy apples and crust - enjoying each and every bite. She thought, "Today is a good day!"

After a short time Bobby looked up at his father. "How about your day? How was it?"

His father swallowed the last bite of his apple cobbler. "I heard about a job in Jackson today. It seems they need someone with my background. I'll give them a call tomorrow, and see what it is about." He looked at Bobby and his wife without any reaction. "It can't hurt."

Bobby's mother broke the silence at the table. "How about some help guys with the dishes?" His mother washed, as his father dried the dishes. Bobby placed them back on the shelf in the cabinet. Soon, everything was completely cleaned up.

His father looked at the clock on the wall. He would have to leave for his night job pretty soon. "Bobby. Do you have your homework done?"

"Just about," answered Bobby. "I have to read a short story for tomorrow."

"Better get after it." Bobby's dad spoke in a firm voice.

"Okay," answered Bobby. He knew there would be no putting off his homework. "I'll see you at breakfast." Bobby walked over to his father and gave him a huge hug, turned and walked back down the stairs to his bedroom.

"I'd better get to work." Bobby's father walked slowly to the front door, slipped his coat back on, and turned to say goodbye to his wife. "I'll be back in a few hours." He stepped out the door into the cold night, buttoned his coat shut, took an old stocking hat out of his pocket, and pulled it down over his head. He looked back at his wife standing on the porch by the door. "Looks like more snow on the way."

"I think your right," answered his wife. "Be careful."

"I will." Bobby's father walked through the broken gate carefully, and placed both hands in his pockets to stay warm.

His mother watched Bobby's father walking down the snowy street until he disappeared around a corner several blocks from their house. She knew it would be a cold walk to and from work - they just couldn't afford the extra gas for the car. If he walked fast, he would get there in about an hour. Bobby's mother looked up into the sky, just as the first snowflakes began to fall. She opened the door, looked down the street one final time, and walked back into the house.

Bobby's father bundled up as best he could, and walked briskly down the street. He looked up into the sky for just a moment at the giant snowflakes beginning to fall to the ground. It reminded him of a night a year ago, when the whole family had stood in the middle of their yard eating large giant white snowflakes as they fell. Bobby's father smiled, as he remembered the snowball fight, which came next. He could still hear their laughter in his mind. His father would give just about anything to have those days back again.

Bobby looked up from his homework to the giant yellow apple in front of him on the table. He reached out with his hand, picked up the yellow apple, and looked at it closely. Bobby was sure his grandfather must have looked for a long time for this one very special apple. It was absolutely perfect. Bobby was already imagining how juicy it would taste. He pushed back his chair, walked up the stairs to the kitchen, found a knife, and cut it in half. Each half looked delicious.

He walked into the living room, where his mother was sitting on the couch knitting something new.

She looked at the new slippers on Bobby's feet. "How do they feel?"

"They're great!" answered Bobby. "And really warm!" He could see that this made his mother really happy. "Here." Bobby handed half of the giant yellow apple to his mother.

His mother took the half of apple from Bobby, as he sat down on the couch beside her. She smiled at her son. Both of them took a bite of the tasty fruit at the same time. The juice of the delicious yellow apple squirted out of their mouths and down their chins at the same time. It was so good!

After a few more bites, Bobby and his mother finished each half of the special apple. "Can I watch television for a few minutes?"

"Sure," said his mother. "But only one show, then its time for bed."

Bobby turned on the television. The images on the screen were not clear, but something was, better than nothing.

His mother went back to her knitting as Bobby settled in on a show. When the show was nearly over, Bobby changed to the other channel quickly. He looked at his mother to see if she had noticed.

"Nice try!" His mother never looked up from her knitting. "Off to bed. I will be down in a little while. We have a poem to read!"

Bobby smiled and turned off the television.

His mother continued to knit.

Bobby was pretty sure she would continue to knit until his father came home from his night job. "What are you making?"

"A new scarf for your father." She held up a small section of the scarf. She was making it from blue and red yarn that she had saved a long time ago. "It will help him stay warm when he walks to work."

Bobby grumbled to himself as he headed down the stairs to get ready for bed. He was already thinking about another day at school and those mean kids. Bobby quickly undressed and pulled on an old sweatshirt and sweatpants for pajamas. The basement would cool off in the middle of the night, as they turned down the heat at night to conserve fuel. Bobby pulled back the heavy blankets and crawled under them. They were always cold for the first few minutes, and then they would warm up after his body was in there for awhile. He listened to his mother's footsteps across the floor and down the stairway.

"So..." said his mother. She pulled up the chair next to the bed. "We are going to read some Robert Frost tonight."

Bobby watched as his mother picked up the old book and turned each page carefully, until she reached the very first selection of poems. His mother began to read the poem with feeling and passion, as Bobby pictured every word in his mind. His mother closed the book gently after a while and placed it carefully on the table.

"Goodnight." Bobby's mother leaned over him, and kissed him on the forehead. "How about pancakes for breakfast?"

"Sounds great!" Bobby answered. "I love you."

"I love you!" answered his mother. "See you in the morning." She reached over for the light on the table and turned it off. Bobby watched his mother walk slowly back up the stairs. She turned off the light at the top of the stairs.

The basement was entirely dark. Bobby tried to look around the room, but couldn't see anything. He laid his head back into the pillow, closed his eyes, and listened carefully. There were footsteps in the kitchen – his mom must be doing something to get ready for breakfast. Usually, his mother would get everything out on the counters and the table before she went to bed.

The fan on the furnace made a constant squeak as it ran. Bobby listened to the footsteps above, and then the furnace went silent. Bobby's mother must have turned the heat down for the night. The basement was completely dark – there was no noise in the entire house. Even his mother's footsteps had stopped. She must be knitting in the living room.

The silence was difficult for Bobby. He didn't worry about monsters in the dark, but the darkness and silence was always hard for him. Bobby's mind replayed the incident in the bathroom with the red hair boy and his buddy. He wondered why those girls had made fun of his coat. Over and over he kept asking himself, "Why do people hurt each other?" It just didn't make sense to him, "Why would a person make someone else feel bad to make them feel good?" he seemed confused, "Why weren't the other students willing to help me? Was it because I was new? Was it about my clothes?"

Bobby's eyes opened wide. He found the light switch in the dark, reached for his notebook, and began to feverishly write in it.

"Bobby!" shouted his mother down the stairway. "Turn your light off and go to sleep!"

"I'll turn it off in just a moment!" Bobby shouted back. "I'm just finishing writing in my journal."

"That's fine," she answered back. "But I want that light off in ten minutes."

"It will be." Bobby was glad for the extra minutes. His pen was writing as fast as it could go.

The hours went by slowly. Bobby's mother continued to look up at the clock every few minutes or so. Finally, she heard footsteps outside the door. She watched the doorknob turn gradually and the door open slowly. Her husband stepped into the room. He was covered in white snowflakes across his head and shoulders.

"It is really snowing tonight," said Bobby's father as he shook the snow flakes from his body. "There will be some snow on the ground in the morning."

"Let's turn up the furnace a little bit tonight," said Bobby's mother.

Bobby's father agreed it was best to keep the house a little warmer tonight. "The night boss talked to me tonight." He looked at his wife with a familiar look of despair. "He said there is only enough work for a few days more." He shook his head sadly and looked down at the floor. "Things are going to get harder."

"We'll just have to make do with what we've got." She walked over to his side and placed her hand on his shoulder to reassure him. "We'll be okay."

Bobby's father needed to hear her words. "I got paid tonight." He placed a folded up envelope in his wife's hand. "Go get Bobby a new winter coat."

Bobby's mother closed her fingers around the envelope. She knew her husband was right. Their son had to have a new winter coat to stay warm. "I will walk to the store tomorrow and see what I can find." She looked back down at the envelope. Every dollar seemed so precious. She would try to find a good buy on the coat and get Bobby a pair of shoes as well.

The next morning Bobby dressed quickly and ran up the stairs. He could smell the pancakes cooking on the stove. Bobby was secretly hoping the new snow had cancelled school. "Are they closing school today?"

"No." said his mother casually. She was standing at the stove turning pancakes. "There wasn't enough on the ground." She saw a look of disappointment in Bobby's eyes. His mother wondered what was going on. She knew Bobby had always enjoyed going to school. This was very strange indeed. His mother looked at her husband drinking coffee.

Bobby's father had seen the disappointment as well. "How about I walk you to school on my way to work?"

Bobby's eyes lit up. "That would be great!" Bobby sat down at the table, and began to eat one pancake after another. He pushed his chair away from the table and looked at his father. "Are you ready to go?"

Bobby's father looked at his wife with a smile. "Sure!"

The two walked into the living room and put on their coats. "Do you have everything for school?"

Bobby was so excited to walk with his father, that he had left his books and things downstairs. He ran across the living room and downstairs – picked up his things, and ran back to his father waiting by the door.

His mother gave them both a hug and a kiss and sent them on their way. She watched her guys as they walked through the old gate and turned down the sidewalk toward school.

Bobby and his father walked quietly side by side for several blocks.

"Is everything alright at school?" Bobby's father never beat around the bush; he just said what was on his mind.

"It's tough being new," answered Bobby slowly. "It will be okay." Bobby knew his father had enough worries – he sure didn't need another.

"Are you sure?" His father turned Bobby to look him in the eyes.

"I'm sure Dad," answered Bobby. "Today will be a great day."

The two walked together quietly the rest of the way to school. Bobby's father hugged him tightly to his chest. "I will see you after work." His father watched from the street corner as Bobby walked toward the front doors of the school – he pulled his coat tighter around his body and turned toward the direction of his job. Bobby's father kept thinking about his son as he walked down the street. "If only I could find a way to make things better!"

Bobby walked up the stairs of the school to the front doors. He looked back to make sure his father was out of sight, then stepped to the side of the door, folded his arms around his body to stay warm, and waited for the first bell to ring.

CHAPTER 4

Fireball

Bobby continued to look down at his feet and ignored the students walking in the doors of the school. Most of the students were talking about the snow last night, and never paid any attention to him. Just like Bobby, many had hoped there would be enough snow in the morning to cancel school. Instead, the ground had only a thin, white blanket on it, not enough to cancel school. Bobby looked up into the dark skies, wondering if it might snow during the day.

The bell finally rang, signaling kids to hurry to class. Bobby slipped in the door behind a couple of boys walking together. He looked at the bathroom door not far away. He wouldn't make that mistake two days in a row. Bobby was pretty sure Johnny would be looking for him in there.

Suddenly, Bobby was bumped into from the side. "Hey there!" Tim was standing right beside him with his usual big grin.

"Hi," returned Bobby. He couldn't help but stare at Tim. His clothes were a mess – in fact his whole body looked a mess. How could a brother and sister be such opposites? Bobby's eyes looked down at his socks. They looked like the same ones he was wearing the day before.

Tim saw Bobby looking down. "Yep! I'm still wearing my lucky socks." He pulled up his pant legs just enough to prove that he was wearing them. "Want a whiff?" Tim broke out laughing.

Bobby smiled at Tim, "I think I'll pass on that one."

"Are you sure?" Tim was obviously teasing Bobby.

Bobby smiled and continued walking down the hallway with Tim at his side. He never had a chance to say a word, as Tim continued to talk non-stop.

"Have you seen Johnny around?" asked Tim. "It would be best to avoid that guy as much as possible."

"I have been," answered Bobby. "What's his problem?"

"Johnny has always been a bully. I have been in classes with him since we were in the first grade." Tim looked at Bobby. "He's a bully!"

"What about Brad?" asked Bobby. "Is he a bully also?"

"No," replied Tim. "Brad is a follower. He's actually a pretty good guy when he is away from Johnny." Tim continued, "Brad and I hung out together for awhile last summer when Johnny was gone. He was a lot of fun to be around."

Bobby and Tim walked to the door of Mr. Reed's class, and went quietly down the side of the room to their desks. Bobby glanced sideways for an instant – there was no sign of Johnny or Brad.

Mr. Reed was standing near the back of the room pinning some papers on the wall. "Good morning boys." He gave Tim that look that said, "Don't mess around in my class today."

Tim seemed to understand the look. "Good morning Mr. Reed."

Bobby replied, "Good morning."

Mr. Reed looked next at Bobby. "Good to see you in the room a little earlier today."

Bobby didn't know whether to smile or not at his comment. He looked back down at his things and placed them on top of his desk.

Mr. Reed's eyes darted from Tim and Bobby to the front of the room. Brad was standing by the teacher's desk nervously awaiting Mr. Reed. Johnny entered the doorway at that same moment. Johnny gave Brad a mean look, and then smiled at Mr. Reed walking toward him. Brad was even more nervous with Johnny near him.

The teacher took Brad and Johnny back into the hallway. Most of the students in the classroom watched while Mr. Reed spoke quietly to the boys for a couple of minutes.

Brad walked back into the room by himself – at the same time, Mr. Reed continued to talk with Johnny outside the door. Brad went quietly to an empty desk across from Bobby without saying anything. He sat down, took out his things, and placed them on the desk - never looking at anyone.

"Brad!" whispered Tim. "What's going on?"

Brad looked back at Tim. "Mr. Reed told me to behave and sit here."

"What did your parents do last night?" Tim

figured Brad was in a lot of trouble at home. His dad was very strict with Brad.

"My dad was really angry. I have to do a bunch of stuff at home and cannot be near Johnny anymore." Brad took a deep breath. "Johnny was pretty upset when I told him last night on the phone. He told me it was my fault that we got caught." Brad took a deep breath. "He'll probably start picking on me again."

"Hey!" Tim placed his arms out wide with a big grin on his face. "I'll be your bodyguard!"

The thought of scrawny Tim protecting Brad made him laugh softly. "Thanks. That's all I need – Tim the Bodyguard." Brad's eyes looked seriously at Bobby. "Watch out. Johnny is after you."

"Why?" whispered Bobby back.

"There is never a reason why he picks on people," said Brad. "He just enjoys being a bully. Stay away from him."

Bobby nodded his head as he looked at Brad. He thought, "Tim's right. Brad is okay."

Mr. Reed finished talking in the hallway with Johnny, and told him to go sit down at his desk.

Johnny stepped into the room through the doorway for a second and looked around with a big grin on his face. He was making sure the other students in the room were watching him. Johnny's eyes came to an abrupt stop at Bobby. The two stared at each other for a moment. Johnny mouthed the words, "You're mine!"

Bobby felt a chill go up and down his spine, and then he looked back down at his things on the top of the desk.

The red hair boy walked to his desk with his usual strut and sat down in the chair. He turned around and looked back at Bobby one last time. Bobby was looking down at his things.

Many of the other students in the room saw it happen. Tim tapped Bobby on the shoulder from behind. "This isn't good."

"I know," said Bobby without looking up. He sat there wondering what Johnny was planning.

"Yesterday," said Mr. Reed in a loud voice. "I asked you to read the story beginning on page 121. Let's talk about it for a little while." He looked around the room. "Shaun. What was this story about?"

Bobby was trying to listen to Shaun, but he kept thinking about Johnny. He looked up at the clock on the wall – it seemed like the second hand of the clock was barely moving. Bobby stared at the back of Johnny's head, as he tried to think of a way to get past him at the end of class.

The minutes dragged on and on, and the class finally ended. Bobby had barely heard a word during the entire class. He was only focused on Johnny, and how to avoid him at the end of class.

The bell rang and all the students stood up. Everyone began to leave the room – except one. Johnny remained in his seat. This was a great opportunity for Bobby to get out of the room before Johnny could leave. He was surprised to see Brad hurrying out of the room right beside him. Bobby could hear Mr. Reed talking to Johnny as he passed by.

"You were better behaved in class today." He placed his hand on Johnny's shoulder. "I will see you after school again tonight." said the teacher. "Tonight will be your last night of detention."

It was just enough time for Bobby and Brad to disappear around the corner into the hallway filled with students. Brad looked at Bobby, "Where are you heading?"

"Gym." answered Bobby. "It's my first class today. Do you know who the teacher is?"

"Mr. Nelson." said Brad, as he came to a stop by a classroom door. "He's mean!" Brad smiled at Bobby, as he turned to walk into a classroom. "Don't get in his way!"

Bobby continued walking toward the gym. His mind kept thinking about what Brad had just said. He opened the gym door slowly and saw most of the class sitting on a long bench against the wall. Bobby walked over to a short man dressed in a red tee shirt and black shorts. Even his shoes were color-coordinated. He was looking down at some papers on his clipboard. Bobby noticed that his whistle and cord around his neck were red and black as well.

"I'm Bobby." He waited for some kind of response. There was nothing. Bobby continued to stand in front of the teacher without moving. He was getting more nervous with each passing second.

Mr. Nelson finally looked up from his clipboard. His eyes scanned Bobby from head to toe. He looked carefully at the old worn out coat in his arms to the shoes with holes in the toes.

"Do you have a better pair of shoes than this?" The teacher stared at Bobby's feet with a frown on his face.

"No sir." replied Bobby. "These are all that I have." He looked down at his shoes.

"Great!" said Mr. Nelson indignantly. He pointed to a large box at the opposite end of the gym. "Find a pair in that box to wear for class – and don't walk off with them after class! You understand me?"

"Yes sir." answered Bobby, as he walked slowly past all the students sitting. One by one each boy on the bench would watch Bobby as he walked by them. All of them knew he was going to the box for a pair of old shoes. Bobby was very embarrassed! He reached the box and looked inside. It was full of shoes that had been worn by someone else previously. The shoes were just piled on each other. Most were dirty and smelled terrible. It was very difficult to see a matched pair – let alone a pair that fit his feet. Bobby found two old shoes that were a match. They were slightly bigger than his feet, but he would make them work. Bobby placed the shoes under his arm and returned to the benches with the rest of the class.

Bobby's eyes glanced down the bench at all of the boys in the class. He saw a familiar face sitting by himself. Jamal was reading a book. He seemed to be ignoring everyone around him.

Bobby sat down beside Jamal. "Hi." He began to take off his shoes and put on the borrowed shoes from the box. Bobby lifted one of the borrowed shoes up to his nose. "The smell is disgusting."

Bobby slipped both his feet into the borrowed shoes, and began to tighten the shoestrings. He tried not to think about whom else had worn the shoes before him.

Jamal looked up from his book. "Bobby!" He seemed genuinely happy to see him. "How's it going?"

"Okay." replied Bobby as he tied the last shoestring in a knot. "What are you reading?"

"Johnny Tremain," answered Jamal. "It's a story about the American Revolution and a group called the Sons of Liberty. I just started it."

Bobby seemed to sit up a little straighter. "That's strange," said Bobby. "My ancestors were some of the first in America – and were members of the Boston Sons of Liberty."

"Really?" Jamal wanted to hear more. He placed a bookmark in the book. He immediately wanted to ask Bobby a hundred questions. "What..."

The silence of the gym and students talking softly to each other was broken by a long loud shrill of a whistle. Bobby's eyes looked to the center of the gym floor, where Mr. Nelson stood with his feet apart and a hand on each of his hips. There was clearly no expression of happiness on his face.

"Stand on the line!" His voice seemed to echo throughout the gym. "Move it!"

All of the boys sitting on the benches quickly jumped to their feet, ran to the line, and stood at attention. Bobby followed the others with Jamal beside him.

"Count off in sixes!" shouted the teacher, as he looked at the first person in the line by the doors. "Speak up nice and loud!"

"One!" shouted the first boy.

"Two!" shouted the next student.

A tall boy shouted, "Three!"

And so it went, "Four! Five! Six! One! Two!"

Bobby tried to anticipate what his number was going to be. Finally, the boy next to him shouted, "Six!"

Bobby was extremely nervous. He shouted, "Seven!" Bobby had no idea how it happened. The frown on Mr. Nelson's face grew even greater. "I'm sorry!" He quickly corrected the number. "One!"

Mr. Nelson didn't look like the forgiving type. His cold eyes seemed to stare right through Bobby's face. The gym teacher blinked his eyes a couple of times and turned slightly toward Jamal.

"Two!" shouted Jamal next to Bobby. He looked at Bobby and took a deep breath. Jamal knew it was a bad idea to make this teacher angry.

Mr. Nelson waited for each student to call out a number. He stood perfectly still for several seconds before saying a word. His cold eyes stared at each boy down the line. "When I blow the whistle, you will proceed to the line of your number." The teacher walked to the front of the gym. "The one's will line up here!" Nelson walked a few more steps across the front of the gym. "The two's will line up here!" He continued to walk across the gym showing each group where to line up. "Then you will turn sideways with your arms extended out making sure you can not touch any person on either side of you." The teacher walked back to the center of the gym. "When you are done – you will face the front of the gym without saying even one word. There will be no talking!"

Mr. Nelson stared at each boy down the line. The boys watched the teacher as he slowly brought the whistle up to his mouth. Mr. Nelson took a deep breath as if he were in slow motion, and then blew hard through the whistle. A loud shrill sound echoed throughout the gym.

The boys ran in every direction looking for their lines. Bobby was sure a couple of them had forgotten their numbers in the panic. Bobby moved out only a few steps and was quickly in the ones line. Each boy turned sideways to make sure they couldn't touch each other. Last, they turned to the front of the gym, and stood quietly while the other lines scrambled to get organized.

The teacher watched each line very closely. His eyes went immediately to the fives line. They were having trouble with their spacing. His whistle sounded out – scaring the death out of everyone. The students in the gym froze. "Fives!" His voice echoed off the walls. "Ten laps around the gym!"

The boys in the fives line quickly left their places and ran around the gym as fast as they could. At the end of the tenth lap, they returned to their places gasping for air– only this time there was no problem with the spacing.

"Jumping jacks!" shouted the teacher. "Twenty five! I want to hear each of you!"

Bobby looked straight ahead at the people in his line. Each of them was trying to get in time with each other. Soon, not only were the ones in time together – but all the lines as well. The count was going pretty well.

"Twenty-three! Twenty-four! Twenty-five!" shouted all the boys in the gym. Bobby's line all stopped together.

"Twenty-six!" Shouted several boys in the fives line. There were a few groans and a bunch of giggles in the other lines.

Mr. Nelson stared at the boys in line five. His eyes seemed to squint even tighter. The veins on his neck began to bulge. "Fives!" the teacher shouted. "Do it again!" The teacher walked down the line staring in the eyes of each boy. The students in the other lines stood quietly and watched line five do the jumping jacks again. This time, each boy finished the count together.

Bobby found himself glad, that he wasn't in line five. He looked over at Jamal in the next line. Jamal looked like he was thinking the same thing.

The teacher worked his way through the different lines. "Push-ups!" His voice seemed to be getting louder. "On your stomachs!"

The kids quickly dropped to the floor, lay on their stomachs, and placed their hands flat on the floor beside their bodies. This was not their favorite exercise.

"Up!" Nelson was standing right beside Bobby's body. He could feel his eyes peering right through him, as he struggled to push up. The teacher knelt down beside Bobby, and shouted loud enough for everyone to hear. "You may wonder how many push-ups we are going to do today? Well... we are going to do push-ups until I get tired!"

The arms of the boys all around the gym started shaking from holding up their bodies for so long. Bobby's arms shook as well. A couple students dropped to the floor, but got back up as soon as they saw the teacher's eyes staring at them with that ugly scowl.

Nelson seemed to enjoy watching the pain in their faces. "Down!" No sooner had their stomachs touched the floor and he shouted again, "Up!" A sick smile crossed his face as the arms of the kids began to shake uncontrollably. "Down!"

The students crashed to the floor. Many were gasping for air or rubbing the muscles on their arms.

"So!" shouted Nelson. "Two is all we can do today!" The teacher walked across the gym staring down at the boys on the floor. "On the next class you will do three – maybe even four!"

The thought of it made several students groan loudly. Bobby was already dreading the next class – but so was everyone else in the room.

Mr. Nelson continued to take the whole class through the rest of the exercises. Even the fives kept up.

"Everyone back on the line!" shouted the teacher. He blew his whistle one loud blast. The entire class ran as fast as they could back to the line. Everyone stood there quietly facing the teacher, waiting for directions.

"We are going to play 'Fireball' today!" shouted Nelson to the class. "We will count off in twos!"

Suddenly, kids were looking down the line and changing their order. The strange thing was – Nelson didn't seem to care!

Bobby was a two. He looked down the line and saw that Jamal was also a two. He didn't know what 'Fireball' was, but at least he had a new friend on his team.

Nelson told the ones to go to one end of the gym and the twos to the other. The teacher walked over to the side of the floor beside the benches. "If you are hit by a ball, you are out unless someone on your team catches a ball in the air before it touches the floor. If you catch a ball, you can choose whom ever you wish on your team to step back on the floor." The teacher opened a large canvas bag by the bench, and turned it upside down. Small red rubber balls the size of a hand rolled out on the floor.

Jamal moved next to Bobby and spoke softly to him. "Let an easy one hit you, so you can get out of the game."

"Okay." Bobby wondered what was going on.

It was pretty obvious that a certain type of kid was on each team. The ones all looked like kids that could really throw the ball hard. The twos all looked like kids – that were 'throwing challenged'.

The teacher blew the whistle. Everyone on the ones ran as fast as they could for a rubber ball. A couple of kids on the twos team ran for some balls near the front line. Several balls immediately hit them, as they tried to pick up the red rubber balls. Bobby could see it was not a good idea to go near the front line.

Bobby watched as another boy on his team was hit hard on the arm. A red welt puffed up immediately in the spot. Bobby backed up to the rear line away from the throwers on the other team. He was thankful they couldn't cross the half court line of the gym and get closer. Bobby felt Jamal brush into him as he ran by him.

Jamal took an easy one in the side of his body and left the floor. He gave Bobby that look to do it also.

Bobby was thinking about doing it, when he felt the impact of a red rubber ball slightly hitting him in the neck. He felt the skin go numb and then the stinging that followed. Bobby heard a voice from the ones at the center of the floor. "I got the new kid!"

The game continued for only a few more minutes before the ones hit the last two kids.

Everyone back up!" shouted Nelson from the bench. "There is only time for one more game." He looked at both teams. "If I blow the whistle two times in a row – you can cross the other team's line."

The ones laughed and joked with each other. The twos seemed to be outright frightened of this new rule. Nelson blew his whistle and the game started again.

Bobby took Jamal's advice this time and barely got hit. He stood on the side watching the game with interest. It appeared the ones were trying not to hit Jamal. It wasn't long until Jamal was the only kid left on the twos team. The fear on Jamal's face was easy to see. He went to the back of the court and picked up several balls and threw them weakly back at the other team. The boys on the ones team caught many of the balls and got all their team back on the floor. It wasn't long before the ones team had all the balls.

At that precise moment the sound of a loud whistle blew twice. The ones realized they could cross the half court line – and so did Jamal! The ones ran within feet of Jamal and threw all the balls at the same time. Jamal used his arms to protect his face, but the rest of his body was hit over and over.

Nelson blew the whistle one long last time. "The game is over! Get ready for the bell!"

The ones walked away from Jamal, who was still hunched over at the far end of the room. He stood up straight, wiped the tears from his eyes, and walked back to the bench by Bobby.

Bobby stared at the red spots all over Jamal's body. He was sure there was more under his clothes.

Mr. Nelson walked over to Bobby. "Make sure you put those shoes back in the box! I can't have you walking off with them." The teacher looked at Jamal trying to fight back the tears from getting hit so hard by the balls. "Be tough!"

Jamal never looked up at the teacher; instead he continued to stare at the floor.

Bobby began to untie his shoestrings slowly, as he listened to the sounds of pain coming from Jamal next to him. He took the shoes off and slipped on his old worn out ones, stood up, walked the other shoes back to the box, and threw them inside. Bobby returned to Jamal.

"How about we go to lunch?" Bobby sat down beside him.

Jamal nodded his head yes, but never looked up or said a word.

The bell rang and all the boys in the class began to leave immediately. Many started retelling the story of how they hit Jamal. A couple of boys looked their way and laughed.

Bobby and Jamal walked side by side without saying a word to each other. He knew Jamal was still hurting. Somehow, they had beat most of the students to the lunchroom. There was no line of students waiting to get food. The two boys got their trays and started down the counter with all the food. One of the cooks glanced at the boys, and took a second look at Jamal. The spots on his body were still red. The look on Jamal's face told her everything.

The two boys went to a table at the far corner of the room. Jamal finally broke the silence, "You were telling me about your ancestors in Boston?" He clearly wanted to talk about something else.

"My family came over on the first ships from England to Massachusetts Bay Colony in the 1600's. As time went by, one of their grandsons came to live in Boston. He was a member of the Sons of Liberty."

Jamal was truly interested in what Bobby was saying. You could see his brain thinking about it very carefully. "Tell me more."

"The Sons of Liberty were a secret group organized to stop the bad things the English were doing to the people in the colonies," said Bobby.

"So…" said Jamal, as his brain began to think. "They were like a group of people organized to stop the bullies!"

"I never thought of it that way," answered Bobby. "You're right."

Jamal took a bite of food and chewed it slowly. "We need to start our own Sons of Liberty." He continued to think as he took another bite.

Bobby noticed Tim coming through the line with Brad. He waved his hand at them.

Tim saw Bobby waving at the far end of the room. He nudged Brad. "Let's go sit with Bobby and Jamal."

"Sure," said Brad nervously. The two boys joined Jamal and Bobby at the table.

Brad kept watching the line for Johnny and ate hurriedly. "I don't want to be here when Johnny arrives. He told me last night that he was going to hurt me for ratting on him."

At that moment, Johnny walked into the lunchroom. He scanned the tables until he saw Brad sitting with the Bobby, Jamal, and Tim. Johnny and Brad stared at each other for a moment. Brad looked back down at his food, as Johnny started to move slowly across the room toward him. Johnny looked around to see if other students were watching.

"Look what we have here!" said Johnny as his eyes went from Brad to the other boys, and then stopped on Bobby.

Bobby placed his hands in front of him and stared back. Johnny suddenly became aware that Tim, Jamal, and Brad were also staring back at him.

"Hi guys!" It was Liz's voice. "Mind if we join you?"

Bobby looked into the grinning face of Liz. Behind her was Stephanie standing there - smiling as well.

The girls sat down and stared at Johnny.

Johnny seemed confused as to what was going on. He looked back at Brad. "So these are your new friends?" Johnny tried to look intimidating at each one - especially at Bobby. "Think they can protect you?" Johnny turned and walked away from the group.

"Do you think he is having a bad hair day?" said Tim in a teasing way. Everyone in the group broke into laughter.

Johnny turned back around to see what was going on, but each of them had wiped away their grins and sat there staring at him without emotion. Finally, he turned back around and got back into the lunch line.

"What are you guys up to?" said Liz. "It's got to be something good." She had that look on her face like Tim that reminded you of trouble."

"Nothing," answered Bobby quietly. "Nothing at all."

Jamal continued to look down at his plate. "We're going to start our own Sons of Liberty." Jamal looked up into the interested faces of the group and told them what Bobby had said. "We are going to fight back in our way! This meanness has to stop!"

"You can't call yourselves the Sons of Liberty," said Liz, as she leaned forward to get everyone's attention.

"Why?" replied Bobby.

"You'll have to be called the Sons and Daughters of Liberty!" Liz puffed up as she emphasized 'daughters'. "I'm in."

Stephanie looked at Bobby with a smile, "Me too."

"I'm in," said Jamal and Tim together.

Everyone looked at Brad. "I don't know." He was genuinely scared. "I'm afraid that Johnny will find out and beat me up."

"No one will find out," answered Bobby. "The only people that will ever know will be the members of SDL."

"What is SDL?" asked Liz.

"The Sons and Daughters of Liberty!" answered Bobby.

"We need a leader," whispered Tim. "I think Bobby should be our leader." Everyone agreed.

"No!" Bobby spoke emphatically. "Each of us will be members of the committee for SDL. The majority rules on any decision." Bobby hesitated for a moment. "We can not be in favor of violence and hurting others – otherwise we will become like them. Agreed?"

"Agreed!" Tim spoke in a serious tone. He looked at the others to see if they agreed also. "The committee has made their first unanimous decision."

Jamal was truly the thinker. "How do we stop the bullies and the other mean people in the school?"

"We become the good guys!" Tim said with a laugh. "We will become super heroes! Only members of SDL will know our true identity."

Bobby's Story

"We need our own newspaper," said Bobby. "We will place copies all over the school for kids to read."

A quiet voice spoke up. "It's time to stand up for what is right and get rid of what is wrong." The voice was Stephanie. "And that includes our friends."

Everyone in the group knew she was talking about Maria and Whitney.

"I will do my part," said Stephanie, as she watched the reactions of the others. She saw Bobby smiling at her, and felt better.

"We need a symbol for SDL. It needs to be on everything we do." said Jamal. "Some of the early flags of America had snakes and things on them."

"Snakes!" said Stephanie. "I hate snakes." She smiled at Bobby and Jamal. "Sometimes, I hate frogs also!"

The group laughed. Most of them had heard about the frog incident the day before.

"The original symbol on the Boston flag was a tree," said Bobby. "Our symbol has to be greater than that. It needs to be bright and colorful – it needs to be the colors of liberty."

Jamal spoke quietly, "It should be the symbol of a flag that is bright blue with red stripes. In the left corner of the flag should be three giant letters written in Old English 'SDL'."

The entire group thought it was a good idea.

Jamal looked around the group, "We need a planning meeting as soon as possible." He thought for moment. "Let's meet at the city library on Saturday morning - no one ever goes there." He looked into the faces of the group. Each of them was nodding their head in agreement.

"What an unusual group if I do say." Mr. Roberts was standing behind the group. "What are you up to?"

Bobby spoke up quickly, "We were talking about the American Revolution."

"Yeah!" said Jamal. "Did you know that Bobby's ancestors were some of the first settlers in America?"

"No. I did not know that." Mr. Roberts continued to look carefully at each one of them. He thought, "Good kids, but they are up to something." He started to walk away from the group, then turned around and stared at Bobby. "The price of freedom is commitment." Roberts turned back around, and walked on to the next table and group of students.

"Does he know?" asked Brad.

The group was stunned. "He couldn't know?" said Jamal.

"No way," answered Liz.

All eyes of the group watched Roberts, as he walked away. They looked at each other and laughed.

CHAPTER 5

Basement Tag

The rest of the day went well. Bobby, Brad, and Tim had agreed to meet after school by the school's front door and walk home together. They were well aware of the old saying, 'There's safety in numbers.' The group talked quietly about SDL as they walked. Even Brad seemed to relax; he knew Johnny was still sitting in Mr. Reed's classroom.

"Can you guys hang out for a little while longer?" asked Tim. "It would be fun to keep talking about SDL. This could be really cool!"

"I have to check in with my mom first," answered Brad. "I'm sure my parents would rather see me with you guys instead of Johnny. Where do you want to meet?"

"Let's go to Bobby's house," answered Tim quickly. "Go home and check in, then let's meet at his house in a half hour." Tim looked at Bobby, "Is that okay with you?"

Bobby was speechless and totally flabbergasted. He never expected anyone would want to come to his house. After a moment Bobby said, "Sure..."

The three boys broke up and went their separate ways. Bobby kept thinking, "They don't have homes like mine. What will they think?" He ran down the street, through the gate, and into the house very quickly. "Mom, I need to talk with you." His eyes looked toward the kitchen.

"I'm right here." His mother was sitting in the chair knitting on his father's scarf. "What's wrong?" She could tell by the look on his face that something was really bothering him.

"I met some new friends today." Bobby was struggling to find just the right words.

"And..." said his mother calmly.

"Some of my friends want to come over for a few minutes," said Bobby, trying not to show his embarrassment. "Is that okay?"

Bobby's mother smiled. "Of course it's okay with me."

"Is there anything..." he just couldn't find just the right words.

Bobby's mother knew exactly what Bobby was thinking. "Go look in the freezer. I picked up a package of Popsicle's at the store today. Offer them to your friends."

"There will be only three of us Mom," answered Bobby. "We'll have just one each." He walked into the kitchen and opened the freezer door of the refrigerator. Inside the freezer was a large bag of Popsicles. The bag had all his favorite flavors – banana, cherry, lime, and root beer. His mom had saved the day again.

Bobby heard a knock at the front door. He closed the freezer door and went quickly to let his friends come in. Bobby stepped back from the door as Tim and Brad entered the room. They were bundled up tight in their coats to keep the cold out.

"You can lay your coats on the chair." He pointed to the chair under the wall hooks for coats.

Brad lay his coat down gently on the chair. Tim yanked his coat off in a hurry and threw it on top of Brad's.

Bobby watched 'messy' Tim in action. "Mom, this is Brad and Tim. We're in classes together at school."

"I'm glad to meet you." Bobby's mother continued to knit as she talked.

"What are you knitting?" Tim nearly sat on her lap to get a better view of the scarf. "That is good looking! Would you make me one? My mom knits sometimes, but she always asks me to go play, when she is doing it!"

"We'll see," said Bobby's mother calmly. "There are some Popsicle's in the kitchen if you boys would like one."

"Sounds great," said Tim, as he quickly left the edge of the chair by Bobby's mother, and was off for the kitchen on his own. "I've got dibs on root beer!" Tim seemed to be himself no matter where he was.

Brad followed Tim calmly into the kitchen. He shouted to Tim already with his head in the freezer. "Do they have banana or cherry? I really like those flavors."

Bobby leaned over his mother and gave her a kiss on the cheek. "Thanks Mom." He turned to join his friends in the kitchen.

Tim had already found a root beer in the bag, when Bobby caught up. "Umm, good!" There was going to be no licking of this Popsicle. Tim was already biting off chunks and digesting them.

Brad was staring at a banana Popsicle in one hand and a cherry in the other. "I just can't make up my mind which one would be better."

Tim stopped his relentless attack of the root beer Popsicle just long enough to take the cherry out of Brad's hand; and handed it to Bobby. "Enjoy!" He returned his attention to the attack on the root beer Popsicle.

Bobby and Brad looked at each other in disbelief, and then broke into laughter. They quickly took the plastic off their Popsicle's and started to attack them as well. It wasn't long before all three boys had cleaned their Popsicle's right down to the two wooden sticks in the middle. Bobby showed the boys where the garbage can was kept under the sink. Brad and Bobby placed their sticks in the garbage can.

Tim held his sticks up in front of his eyes, and examined them closely. "Did you ever wonder why they place two pieces of wood in Popsicle's? Maybe some one was hoping that we would get a sliver on our tongues?" At that moment, Tim started shouting, "Ow! I've got a sliver in my tongue! Ow!" He grabbed his face, as if he were in great pain.

Bobby couldn't decide if he was acting, or if something had really happened. "Are you okay?"

"He's just playing," said Brad calmly. "You never know what Tim is going to do?"

"What's wrong?" Bobby's mother rushed into the kitchen with her knitting needles in hand.

Tim stopped his acting immediately. "Nothing, I was just practicing for a play I'm going to be in."

"When is the play?" asked his mother.

"Next summer," said Tim. "I think?"

Bobby's mother gave him that look, which said it was a good time to go downstairs with his friends.

"Come on guys. Let's go down to my room." Bobby led the way down the stairs with Brad and Tim behind him.

His mother returned to the living room smiling. "Tim!" She sat back down and started knitting again. "He's going to keep life exciting."

Brad and Tim looked around the basement without saying much.

"Do you have any games?" asked Brad.

"Not really." said Booby. He was starting to show some embarrassment. "We got rid of everything when we moved."

Tim's face seemed to change from his usual jokester look, to one of caring and concern. "Why did you move?"

"Both of my parents lost their jobs back home." Bobby took a deep breath. He had never shared any of this with another kid. "We eventually lost our home and almost everything we owned."

Brad and Tim sat down on his bed as they listened to Bobby explain all the bad things of the past. After a few minutes, Bobby stopped talking. He didn't know if he should have told them everything.

"There is one good thing that happened," Tim's mischievous smile grew large on his face. "You found us!" All three boys laughed together.

"I know a game we can play. I played it once at a friend's house," said Brad. "Basement Tag!"

Bobby and Tim almost said it together at the same time, "Basement Tag?"

"Yep!" answered Brad. "The game is played on the floor. Nobody is allowed to stand up or leave the floor. When you touch the other person, then they are 'it'."

"That doesn't sound too fun," said Bobby. "Is that everything?"

"Nope." Brad's eyes started to twinkle. "The game is played in the dark."

"Alright!" shouted Tim almost immediately, "This is my kind of game!"

Upstairs, Bobby's mother heard the word 'alright' from the basement. She smiled and thought, "Tim!"

"The first thing we must do is make sure there is nothing that could hurt us," said Brad.

The three boys moved everything out of the way in the basement that could hurt them in the dark. All of the lights were turned off except the one by Bobby's bed. The door to the stairway was closed tight.

Brad stood by the light switch – ready to turn off the last light for a test. He turned the switch off. The entire room turned into total darkness. Brad turned the light back on. "It will be perfect for the game! I will be 'it' first."

"Cool!" shouted Tim. "Let's get it on!"

"Remember," said Brad. "Once you are tagged, you must go look for the third person. You can not tag the one who tagged you for at least two minutes." Brad looked into the eyes of Bobby and Tim. Their excitement was easy to see. Brad turned off the light.

Each of the boys moved in different directions and dropped to the floor. Bobby crawled to a corner of the room, backed up against the wall, and listened for Brad and Tim moving about.

"Tim!" said Brad in a giggling voice, "I can smell your socks!"

"No you can't!" said Tim without thinking. Tim realized that he had just given away his location to Brad. He tried to move in the opposite direction from Brad's voice, but it was too late.

Brad could hear Tim's body sliding on the floor in front of him. He jumped out into the darkness, "Gotcha!"

Tim not only jumped when Brad jumped on him, but he let out a brief scream. Brad had scared him to death! Tim couldn't believe how scary it was to get tagged in the darkness. He loved this game!

Upstairs, Bobby's mother heard the scream. "They got Tim." She continued to knit.

Brad moved away from Tim quickly. He tried to get to a corner of the room far away from Tim's noises.

Tim stopped crawling on his knees. He could hear Brad moving away, but there was no sound of Bobby in the room. Tim decided to use Brad's trick to find Bobby with a different twist to it.

"B-o-b-b-y," said Tim in a low slow voice. "I'm the ghost of the dark cold basement." Tim began to giggle softly and had to change his voice low again. "I'm going to sneak up on you and..." He hesitated for a moment. "... Grab you!"

Bobby still sat in the corner far away from Tim. He was trying hard not to laugh. He thought, "Tim is so funny!"

Tim turned around and around – trying to hear a noise. He soon forgot which direction was which in the darkness. Tim heard a noise behind him. He scrambled across the floor as fast as he could and pounced into the darkness. It was a direct hit! Tim was proud of himself. "I got you Bobby!"

"Not hardly." It was Brad's voice. "You got me."

"Oops!" Tim couldn't believe that Brad wasn't Bobby. "Sorry!" Tim moved away from Brad, taking his time, as he slid across the floor. "B-o-b-b-y! I'm going to find you. I will change into the super hero, 'Wonder Kid', and turn on my night vision goggles to see you."

Bobby sat in the corner thinking that Tim never shuts up. He decided it was time to attack and not wait to be found. Bobby could hear Tim moving in his direction. He tried to see Tim in the dark, but it was impossible to see anything. Bobby heard Tim slide just a couple feet in front of him. He heard Tim turn around with his back to Bobby.

"I know you're both in here somewhere," said Tim. "Brad. It's been long enough now. I can find you as well." He listened carefully for the slightest noise. There was not one sound in the dark basement. Tim dropped his voice again, "I am the ghost..."

Bobby never let Tim finish his sentence. At that precise second, he jumped out and screamed loudly behind Tim. Tim was so scared that he let out a scream. Brad was in the far corner of the room rolling in the darkness and laughing as hard as he could.

Upstairs, his mother grinned while listening to the screams from below. "Bobby got Tim!" She smiled and continued to knit.

The boys chased each other in the darkness for nearly an hour. Everyone had been 'it' at least a couple of times. Tim was 'it' again and couldn't find Brad or Bobby. He kept talking as usual – trying to get one of the boys to laugh. There was no noise of any kind. Tim searched the floor back and forth in the darkness. He began to get nervous. All of the talk about ghosts had scared him. "This isn't funny," said Tim with a scared tone in his voice. "Where are you guys?"

Tim found the light switch by the bed and turned it on. He looked across the entire room. Nowhere was Brad or Bobby in sight. Thoughts of ghosts crossed his mind for a just a second.

Four hands reached out from under the bed, and grabbed Tim by the ankles. Tim let out another blood-curdling scream!

Bobby and Brad crawled out from under the bed laughing as hard as they could. "You guys..." Tim could see they had gotten him good.

Bobby's mother heard the scream from down in the basement. She stopped knitting and laughed, "They really got Tim this time!"

"I'd better head for home," said Brad. "This was so much fun." He patted Tim on the shoulder. "Great scream."

"Thanks," said Tim. "I'd better go too. I'm supposed to meet my sister out in front in a few minutes. She's been at a friend's house near by."

The three boys walked up the stairs together and still laughing. They had really enjoyed playing 'Basement Tag' together. It would be fun to do it again.

Tim stopped for a moment by Bobby's mother, "Good night Mrs. 'T'. The root beer Popsicle was great!" A large mischievous grin formed on his face. "The screams weren't bad either. I made them think that they scared me, but I was really just fooling them." Tim winked at Bobby's mother.

"Sure," said Bobby's mother. "You fooled them real good – and me too."

Brad thanked her for the Popsicle and fun. "Good night."

"You're welcome boys." His mother knew these were good kids for Bobby to be with.

"Mom, is it okay if I go out front with Tim for a little bit?" said Bobby. "He's waiting for his twin sister."

"Sure," said his mother. "Hmmm – twins?"

Bobby seemed to know what his mom was thinking. "They are actually nothing alike – thank goodness!" He pulled on his coat and followed the boys outside.

Brad said goodbye and took off down the street. He didn't want to get into anymore trouble. "See you tomorrow!"

Tim looked the other way down the street. He could see Liz walking down the sidewalk. "Quick! Cover me up with snow." Tim lay down beside the fence next to some old bushes.

Bobby quickly covered Tim with snow until he couldn't be seen, and then he went to hide around the corner of the house to see what was going to happen next.

Liz walked at a fairly fast pace. She was singing a song softly to herself and looking for Bobby's house. Liz recognized the house number and started to reach for the old gate.

Tim jumped up from under the snow like a crazed wild animal. He was screaming and flailing his arms everywhere.

Liz jumped back - falling onto the snowy ground. Her heart was pounding. Her face finally focused on Tim. There was definite anger in her eyes.

Tim laughed hard at his sister, ran out the gate, and down the street. Liz jumped back to her feet and was right behind him.

Inside the house, Bobby's mother heard the scream of Liz, "Tim got his sister." She sat there and laughed. "Tim is an original!"

Bobby walked back into the house, grinning from ear to ear. "They are running home." He giggled a little bit. "I'm going to do my homework."

His mother continued to smile as she watched Bobby go back down stairs. It was good to see him laughing with friends again.

Bobby finished his homework quickly. He was flipping through the pages of his Literature book when some words on the page caught his attention. He read it out loud, "The pen is mightier than the sword." Bobby's mind thought about the meaning of the words. "Problems should be solved through words – not violence!" It was exactly what he believed.

"Bobby!" shouted his mother down the stairs. "Dad's home. Come on up for dinner."

"Coming!" Bobby shouted back up the stairs. He thought about the words again, "The pen is mightier than the sword." Bobby ran up the stairs to see his father.

Bobby hadn't heard his father come in. He was sitting in the chair - looking more exhausted than ever. "What time do you have to leave for your night job?"

"In about an hour," answered his dad. "How was your day?"

Bobby was excited to tell his dad about his new friends and especially 'Basement Tag'. His father looked up at his wife, who was leaning against the kitchen sink with a big grin on her face.

"You'll have to meet Brad and Tim," said Bobby.

"Especially Tim," said Bobby's mother. Bobby and his mother laughed at the same time. "He's an original." The two laughed again.

Bobby's mother began to place a couple of hot dishes on the table. In one pan was boiled potatoes, and in the other pan was green beans creamed in a white sauce. She placed the bread and butter on the table by Bobby.

"This looks great!" Bobby held up his plate for his mother to serve him. He thought, "At least, we won't have to eat 'Tomatoes Ala Yuk' again tonight."

Bobby's parents looked at each other in surprise. It was nice to see Bobby so happy.

"It looks great!" said his father. "I'm starved."

Bobby dominated most of the conversation during dinner. He told his parents about the tag game. They laughed together as he shared the time when he sneaked behind Tim and scared him. Then, Bobby told them about Tim hiding in the snow and scaring his sister.

Bobby's mother sat back in her chair and watched her husband laugh until tears flowed down his cheeks. It was good to see both of them laughing.

"I think this occasion deserves something special," said his father to his wife. "What do you think?"

"I agree." said his mother. "It is a special day." She walked into the next room and came back with two sacks, and placed them in front of Bobby.

Bobby was confused. It wasn't his birthday. "What's in it?" asked Bobby.

"I guess you will have to open it to find out," said his father with a hint of excitement in his voice.

Bobby reached into the sack and pulled out the cloth inside. It was a brand new dark green and white winter coat. He felt the emotions inside him turning upside down. It was the first new thing he had received since they lost their house back home.

"Put it on," encouraged his mother. "Let's make sure it fits."

Bobby slipped on the coat carefully. It was a perfect fit! He walked over to both of his parents and gave them a huge hug. "Thank you!" Bobby continued to look at the coat as best he could.

"Come on," said his dad. "There's another sack for you to open."

Bobby opened the second sack slowly. What could be better than a new coat? His hand pulled out a brand new boot, and then a second one. Bobby's mind seemed to swirl. He knew his father had worked nights for these things. Bobby hugged his father long and hard.

"One more thing..." said his mother triumphantly. "I have something for all of us." Bobby's mother opened the freezer door. Behind the Popsicles were three ice cream bars. The three of them enjoyed their first ice cream in five months.

Bobby's father lay down on the couch after dinner. He watched Bobby replace his old coat with the new one. The father thought it was strange that Bobby was taking the old coat back down stairs. "What are you doing with the coat?"

Bobby stopped and looked at his father, "This will remind me always where we came from..." He turned around and went down stairs. "And what you did for me."

His father looked at Bobby with great pride, closed his eyes, and fell into a deep sleep. He knew the pain and suffering was worth it.

It wasn't long before his wife shook him gently. "It's time to go to work."

Bobby's father sat up and tried to wake up. He stood on his feet finally. "I expect there will be no more work after tonight."

His mother placed his coat over his broad shoulders. "We'll be fine." She took something from the place where she was knitting. "I finished you a scarf today." She placed it around his neck and face, then helped zip up his coat.

"Feels warm," he said. "Thank you."

"You are very welcome." She reached up and gave him a kiss.

Bobby's father opened the door into the cold night, and began his long walk to work. He would think about all the good things in Bobby's day – and that would make the walk easier.

She closed the door slowly, watching her husband for as long as she could, as he walked down the street into the cold night.

Bobby came wandering up the stairway a short time later. He seemed to have a troubled look on his face, as he sat down on the couch next to his mother.

"Bobby," His mother could see the look of concern on his face, "What's wrong?"

"It's not fair," said Bobby quietly. "I got everything! Dad and you got nothing."

"That's not true." His mother pulled Bobby closer to her. "Your father and I always wanted a good education. He only got to the eighth grade and had to quit. I graduated from high school. You can't have a good future, if you don't have a good education." She continued to talk softly to Bobby. "It is our dream that one day you will go to college and get a good job. We don't want you to ever hurt like this." She played with the curls on his head – this time Bobby didn't seem to care. "Someday you will do it for your children, as we are doing it for you, and they will do it for their children."

Bobby cuddled even closer to his mom. "It just doesn't seem fair."

"It's not fair," said his mother. "Life is not always fair. In fact – sometimes it is down right hard." She continued to hold him tight. "Just remember when you grow up - to always give back what you take from life. Never forget these times, for it is in difficult times like these that we find out what kind of people we really are. Our best always comes forward."

"Like Dad doing two jobs?" replied Bobby.

"Yep!" said Bobby's mother. "There isn't anything he wouldn't do for you."

"I know." answered Bobby.

"When you do your best," said his mother. "Then everything we've gone through is worth it. Do you understand?"

"Yes. I know what you are saying." Bobby nodded his head.

Bobby's mother looked up into the air. She knew things would get better for them, she just wasn't sure how much longer it would be.

Bobby sat back up, and looked at his new coat. "It's beautiful."

"It sure is," answered his mother. "How do the boots fit?"

"Perfect," answered Bobby enthusiastically. "They will definitely keep the cold out." He stood up and looked back down at his mother. "I will never forget this!" Bobby turned to go back down stairs.

His mother felt a lump in her throat and fought back the tears. "I'll be down to see you in a little while."

Bobby wrote down his entire day in his journal. It was strange to actually have a day where most things were pretty good. He spent a great deal of time writing about the coat and the sacrifices made by his father and mother.

The next morning, Bobby took his time putting on his new boots. He stood up and looked down at them. They were brown and shiny – he even looked taller in them.

His father and mother were sitting at the table waiting for the fashion show. "You look taller," said his father.

"They are good looking on you," said his mother. "Turn around."

Bobby turned around and showed his new boots to them. "I'm starved!"

Bobby's mother went to the stove and brought over a plate with a stack of pancakes on it. "I thought you might be." She watched, as Bobby poured maple syrup over the stack and started to devour them.

"Shall we walk to school together?" said his father. "The sky is clear, but it is real cold."

"Do you mind if a friend walks with us?" said Bobby between bites. "Tim is going to meet us down the street." Bobby smiled at his mother.

"Tim?" Bobby's father looked at his wife standing by the counter grinning. "Sure. That will be fine."

"Tim," said his mother with a slight giggle. "He should make your walk go by quickly."

His father looked at her with a puzzled look.

"You'll see!" laughed his wife. "Like I told you – he's an original."

The two guys went to the door and pulled on their coats. Bobby was proud of his new coat. It was so bright – and new! His father looked at his wife and smiled.

"See you after school!" shouted Bobby from the old gate, with his dad right behind him.

His father looked back at his wife and smiled again. They were pleased to see Bobby laughing again.

Bobby and his dad had walked several blocks, but had not seen any sign of Tim. Suddenly, some wild creature from the bushes jumped on Bobby. He nearly fell to the ground from the force.

His father watched this wild creature come to a stop. "Tim?"

"Yes sir!" said Tim with his usual mischievous grin. "You must be Mr. 'T'?" Tim stepped up to Bobby's father and shook hands with him.

"Yep," said Bobby's father with a smile. "This must be Tim."

The three walked on to school together. Tim did almost all of the talking. He talked about playing 'Basement Tag', and how he scared his sister to death.

Bobby looked at his father and smiled. His father said goodbye, left the boys at the corner of the school, and headed for work.

Tim continued to talk non-stop all the way to the front doors of the school and inside the hallway.

CHAPTER 6

The Power of One

Bobby and Tim walked down the hallway together, laughing about the night before. The hallway was crowded with students rushing to class. He felt something hit the side of his foot from behind. The force knocked his foot into the other one – tripping him! Bobby's body flew forward onto the hard tile floor. All of his things scattered in front of him. Bobby was able to get his hands up just in time to protect his face, and just before he slammed into the hard floor.

The students walking by watched Bobby falling, but continued on their way down the hall. No one wanted to get involved or stop to help Bobby – except Tim.

"You stupid jerk!" Tim leaned down to help Bobby back to his feet. He was grabbed by the back of his coat and tossed against a locker. "Ow!"

Bobby turned around to see who had tripped him. Johnny was standing above him with a couple of new friends on each side of him. The mean grin on his red freckled face made Bobby sick.

"I told you guys that I would find you!" Johnny kicked one of Bobby's books down the hallway.

"Oh! By the way..." Johnny looked down at Bobby. "That's a real nice coat. It will look good on me."

Johnny placed his hands on the shoulders of his new buddies and continued walking down the hallway with them. Students passing by continued to look the other way – they were afraid of Johnny.

"That guy is a real jerk," said Tim as he appeared to be exploding at the seams. "Someday..."

"Come on." Bobby began picking up his things off the floor. "We don't want too be late for class." He wasn't crying any longer. There was a new look of determination on his face.

Tim and Bobby stepped into Mr. Reed's classroom just before the bell rang. They walked down the side of the room to their seats without saying a word to each other. Bobby's dark eyes were looking no longer at his feet - now he stared into the faces of students watching him. There was a clear sense of purpose in his walk and face. The students could see it.

Mr. Reed was standing by the windows watching him. He knew something was up, but wasn't sure what it was. He could see the change in Bobby.

Johnny was sitting in his chair talking to a student across from him, and acting as if nothing had happened. Every few moments, he would glance back at Bobby and Tim with his ugly wicked grin.

Bobby took his coat off, set his things on the desk, and stared at Johnny. Bobby thought, "Your time is coming!" He continued to stare at him.

Johnny glanced back at Bobby. Their eyes continued to stare without blinking at each other. Johnny sensed that there was a change in Bobby, which he couldn't quite explain.

Mr. Reed walked down the row of students and stopped beside Johnny's desk. Johnny quit staring at Bobby and turned around. The teacher looked down at him, "You remember our agreement?"

Johnny placed his hands up in front of him, "I'm not doing anything!"

The teacher looked down into his eyes. "I'm sure you're not doing anything." Mr. Reed began to walk backwards very slowly toward the front of the room. He was being careful to keep an eye Johnny. "We are going to get into groups today." He directed the students in the room into five groups. Mr. Reed made sure Johnny was in the group closest to the front of the room and in his eyesight.

Each group in the room quickly formed and awaited Mr. Reed's next direction. Bobby was in a group with Tim, Maria, and Shaun. He purposefully found a seat facing toward Johnny.

"You are going to write a limerick today," said the teacher. "Your limerick needs to be five lines. The first, second, and fifth lines must all rhyme with each other, and the third and fourth lines must rhyme with each other." The teacher showed the class examples of limericks. "You will each write a limerick and share it with your group. You will pick one limerick from your group to share with the entire class." Mr. Reed smiled at the class. "You have thirty minutes to write your limericks."

Bobby and the others in his group started immediately on their limericks. He looked up to the front of the room every once in a while. Johnny sat in his group just watching the others work, never writing a word on his paper. Bobby began to concentrate on his own work.

"Time!" said the teacher after thirty minutes had passed. "Now share your limericks with each other and pick one to represent your group."

Bobby and the others looked at each other. No one wanted to be first.

"I'll do it!" said Tim finally. "You'll like it." He sat up straight in his chair.

Bobby, Maria, and Shaun figured Tim would be up to something. They sat back in their chairs to listen to him.

Tim looked at each of them with a serious look on his face. His famous big grin reappeared, as he began to read his limerick out loud.

"There once was a man named Fred,
Who stabbed himself and bled.
With the knife he played too often,
For now he lies in the coffin,
Poor Fred – is dead."

Bobby and the others were stunned. No one said a word. Suddenly, each of them broke out into laughter.

Mr. Reed walked over to the group and read Tim's limerick to himself. "Tim!" The teacher shook his head and walked over to another group mumbling. "I should have guessed."

Bobby and Shaun each read their work to the group. That left only Maria to do hers. It was easy to see that she was scared to read it. After several seconds, Maria finally began her limerick.

"Winter winds - too cold to fight,
An old coat buttoned up tight.
Never making a sound,
Sad eyes looking down,
No one helping – it's not right!"

Maria continued to look down at her paper with the limerick on it. She glanced at Bobby to see his reaction. The smile on his face told her that it was good.

"Maria's limerick is fantastic," said Bobby. "You read yours to the class." Shaun and Tim agreed.

Maria's limerick was the first to be read in the class. Every student in the room sat in silence – even Johnny. After a few seconds the class clapped their hands for her. Maria's face turned red from embarrassment – only this was the kind of embarrassment she liked. She looked back at Bobby clapping his hands and smiled.

Each group had a chance to share their limerick. It was great to hear all the different ones, but everyone knew Maria's was the best.

It was a fun class today. Mr. Reed looked up at the clock on the wall, "Good job today! Enjoy the weekend, and we'll see you on Monday."

The students began gathering their things and leaving the classroom. Bobby continued to keep an eye on Johnny.

Maria stood up and looked at Bobby. "You have a great weekend." She smiled at him and walked out the door.

Bobby was impressed by Maria's new personality, she was actually nice, and pretty smart when she wanted to be. He pulled his coat back on. Bobby wasn't going to give Johnny any opportunities.

"You ready to go?" It was Tim behind him. "Let's get ahead of that jerk!"

Bobby knew Tim was talking about Johnny. He continued to keep his eyes on the red-haired boy, as he walked up the side of the room with Tim.

Johnny was talking to another student the whole time, and never paid any attention to Bobby and Tim.

"I've got to get to my class early," said Tim nervously. "I didn't finish my homework. I'll meet you for lunch at our table."

Bobby had never thought of it as 'our table'. He looked around for Johnny. There was no sign of him anywhere. Bobby figured it was safe for him to use the bathroom with Johnny still back in the classroom. He walked into the bathroom, set his things on the edge of the sink, and looked into the mirror. Bobby remembered his last encounter with Johnny in this bathroom just a couple of days earlier.

The doors opened slowly. A pair of blue eyes peered inside. Johnny pushed the doors wide open, and strutted into the room with his two new buddies on each side.

Bobby backed up to the sink, keeping his eyes on Johnny.

"I'd really like to have a nice new green and white coat." Johnny stared at Bobby with his cold blue eyes.

One of the boys by his side said, "That coat would look real nice on you."

"Why, you'd look down right pretty," mocked the other boy.

Bobby gritted his teeth and never took his eyes off Johnny. "Leave me alone!" There was no way; he was going to be a victim again to this bully! His dark eyes stared at the red freckles on his face. The fingers on his hands tightened into a clenched fist.

"Oh!" said Johnny in a teasing way. "Is the new boy going to cry?" The two boys and Johnny laughed loudly.

Johnny's grin left his face, as he moved toward Bobby. He could see that something was different, but he still wanted to intimidate him.

The doors of the bathroom opened and several kids walked into the room. It was Brad, Jamal, and Tim.

Johnny looked at the boys and stepped back. He could see that it was no longer three on one. He turned around toward the door and started walking back out with his buddies. "I see you babies all stick together." He laughed again and waved for his buddies to follow him. The three bullies left immediately, trying to act tough and bragging how they scared all the boys.

Bobby looked at his friends in relief. "Thanks." He looked at Tim grinning from ear to ear. "I thought you needed to be to class early?"

"I changed my mind," answered Tim.

"Libertas!" shouted Jamal. "The rallying call to arms!"

Tim looked at Jamal in confusion. "Say what?"

Jamal laughed at Tim. "Libertas is the Latin word for liberty."

Tim turned to Bobby, who was still very serious and determined. "We just thought you needed help."

Bobby and the others walked out of the bathroom together and agreed to meet at lunch – at their table! They broke up and went their different ways to class.

"Thanks guys." Bobby smiled as each went their different ways. He thought, "Libertas!" He turned around and headed for his next class.

A large crowd had formed in the cafeteria when Bobby walked in. He looked toward their table at the far end of the room. Brad and Tim were already seated and waiting for the rest of them. Bobby noticed that Mr. Roberts was standing near by. That was good. Johnny wouldn't try anything with him around.

The smell in the kitchen was great. It was baked chicken with mash potatoes and gravy. Chicken was a huge favorite of the students. There would be a long lunch line. Most students would eat hot lunch today.

Bobby moved slowly in the line. He worked himself to the front of the line eventually. The cooks saw him coming, "Hi Bobby!" said the first cook in the line. "How are you doing?"

"Great." Bobby slid his tray along for the cooks to place food on it. He noticed that the cooks made sure he got the best piece of chicken in the pan and plenty of mashed potatoes and gravy. "Thank you," said Bobby softly. He took his tray heaped with chicken and mashed potatoes, and joined his friends.

"Look at that!" Tim was staring at Bobby's tray of food. "You must be the cooks' favorite?"

Bobby looked down at his tray with a slight smile on his face. He thought, "It's good to be the cooks' favorite."

It wasn't long until Jamal, Liz and Stephanie joined the group. They quickly worked out a time to meet at the city library in the morning.

"Can I join you?" It was Maria standing to the side of the table.

Everyone seemed surprised to see her standing there. Stephanie smiled at her friend, "Sure." Everyone scooted down the bench to make room for Maria.

Tim was fast to tell everyone about the incident in the bathroom and the new word 'Libertas'.

Bobby interrupted Tim and began speak so everyone in the group could hear him, "It's about the power of one!"

The others stopped what they were doing to listen to him.

"What do you mean?" Maria asked, "Explain."

"My grandfather asked me this question a long time ago." Bobby paused for a moment to tell the story like his grandfather. "If someone does something wrong - is it wrong? I told my grandfather wrong is wrong. He asked me if a hundred people did something wrong - is it wrong? I told him that it was still wrong. He asked me if a thousand people did something wrong - is it wrong? I told my grandfather that wrong is wrong no matter how many people did it." Bobby let these thoughts soak in first. He began again, "My grandfather told me that just one person standing up for what is right can be very powerful - but what would happen if others joined that one person?" Bobby had the group not only listening to him, but they were thinking about what he was saying. "This is called the 'Power of One." He looked into the eyes of each person. "Today, we are but a few standing up for what is right - tomorrow we will be more than just a few! The bullies must be stopped."

Every person looked at Bobby in amazement. He had a special way of saying what each person was thinking.

Jamal looked at the size of the group. "We can't meet like this! People are noticing us."

He wasn't the only person to notice the new group sitting together at the back of the room. Mr. Roberts watched them with curiosity. "I wonder what they are doing?"

Bobby saw Roberts staring at the group. Jamal was right. The group was becoming too visible and catching the attention of others. This wasn't good.

"Everyone," Bobby said. "We have to break up!"

Tim and Jamal picked up their trays and went to another table across the room. Bobby and Brad walked back toward the front of the room and sat down at another table. The girls stayed where they were.

Bobby scanned the lunchroom. Everyone had quit watching them – except Roberts! He was still monitoring each of them in their new places. Bobby was sure that he was trying to figure out what was happening.

Johnny eventually walked in with his fellow bullies. They received their food from the cooks, and sat down at a table in the middle of the room. His eyes quickly found Bobby with Brad at a table by themselves. He started to get out of his seat, but felt a hand on his shoulder. Johnny's eyes looked upward into the stern face of Mr. Roberts.

"Done eating already?" asked Roberts.

"No sir!" answered Johnny. "I was just going to sit at another table."

Roberts looked around the room. "The cafeteria is pretty full. Baked chicken is a popular lunch. Looks like you got the best seat in the house." He smiled at Johnny. "You stay here."

Johnny knew that Mr. Roberts wasn't asking - he was telling! Roberts walked away from Johnny to visit with kids at another table. Johnny and his buddies whispered back and forth to each other and looked at Brad and Bobby every few seconds.

"Hi guys!" Mr. Reed sat down with his tray right across from Johnny. "How's the food?"

Kids all across the lunchroom watched as Mr. Reed began to eat his lunch in front of Johnny. There was no doubt about it – Reed and Roberts were taking control of the situation.

Johnny never said another word the entire lunch. It wasn't long before he had finished his food and got up to leave.

Mr. Reed looked up at Johnny with a grin on his face. "You have a great weekend boys." He took another bite of food, and watched Johnny and his friends walk away. Mr. Reed got the attention of Mr. Roberts, who just happened to follow Johnny out of the cafeteria.

As soon as Johnny and Roberts were gone, kids at every table were talking about what they had just witnessed.

Bobby got the attention of the group scattered around the room. He held up his fist with one finger pointing up - the Power of One! Each of the girls held their hands in front of them with one finger pointing up. Jamal, Tim, and Brad did the same. The 'Power of One' was growing!

Mr. Reed noticed the fingers pointing up. He smiled and looked back down at his food, and took another bite.

Bobby and Brad finished their lunches and headed for the library together. They peeked inside the room carefully making sure Johnny wasn't inside. The boys went to a table in the back corner to look at magazines. It wasn't long, before the rest of the group joined them.

"We can not be that obvious again," said Jamal. "People will figure it out."

Everyone agreed that Jamal was right. From now on, they would only meet together as a complete group at the city library - but they would use the 'Power of One' signal to each other. Each of them stood up and began to wander around the library.

Mrs. Wilson watched the group with interest. She wondered what they were up to. Wilson looked up at the clock and warned everyone the bell was about to ring.

"Come on Bobby," said Liz. "We don't want to be late for Roberts' class." The two picked up their things and left quickly.

Mr. Roberts stood at the door greeting each student as they walked into the classroom. "Good afternoon. Good afternoon." It was something he did almost everyday. He smiled as Liz and Bobby walked up to the door. "How is your day going?"

Bobby hesitated for a few moments. "Great!"

"Yes." chimed in Liz. "It is truly a great day."

Bobby and Liz chuckled as they walked past Mr. Roberts into the room.

"Be sure to say 'hello' to Herman," said Mr. Roberts with a small laugh. "He seems a little hungrier today!" He was definitely teasing Bobby.

Bobby looked back at his teacher. He thought, "This man has a great sense of humor." Bobby walked to his seat next to the cage and peered in at Herman. The alligator lay there motionless. Bobby moved closer to make sure Herman was alive. The alligator made one of his famous sounds, making Bobby jump back away from the cage.

"I think Herman misses you." Stephanie sat down at the table with Liz, Jamal, and Bobby. She leaned forward so as not to be heard by other students. "Maria asked if she could come tomorrow to our meeting."

"How did she know?" asked Jamal. He wasn't sure if he could trust Stephanie anymore.

"Bring her," said Bobby without hesitation.

All three of them were surprised by Bobby's quick answer.

Bobby knew they were wondering why he had answer so quickly. "The 'Power of One' must grow! We have to learn to trust each other and forget our differences. Remember, we are few today, but tomorrow we will be many!"

Even Jamal with all his brains, was amazed by Bobby's thinking. "He's right."

Bobby looked back one more time at Herman in the cage. For a moment, he could have sworn that Herman smiled – but alligators can't do that! He looked back into the cage again – Herman was just staring at him - he kind of had that hungry look. Bobby scooted further away from the cage.

Mr. Roberts closed the door. "Take the lids off your frogs." He watched as the students began to take off the lids covering their frogs. "You are going to dissect your frog today." There were many groans in the room and a few quiet cheers.

Stephanie stared at her frog lying in the tray upside down on its back. Her skin began to turn pale. It was easy to see that she was getting sick.

"Mr. Roberts!" Liz got his attention to look at Stephanie.

Roberts could see that she was getting ill again. "Stephanie?" asked the teacher. "I have some papers that need to be taken to the office and a couple of classrooms. Would you mind doing it?"

Stephanie placed the lid back on her frog. "I would be happy to do it." She stood up and picked up the papers from Mr. Roberts and left the room."

Jamal wasted no time dissecting his frog. He began pointing at parts and calling them by names

Liz and Bobby had never heard before. Mr. Roberts was impressed by Jamal's knowledge.

Stephanie walked back into the classroom just as the bell was about to ring. They all walked out of class together.

They were teasing Stephanie about her weak stomach, when they saw Tim coming closer.

"Oh no!" Liz ran to her brother. "What happened to you?"

Tim's body had the familiar red marks on him. A couple marks were actually welting up. "I had gym class today."

Bobby looked at the marks around his face and neck. He knew exactly what had caused it.

Tim went on. "Nelson made us play Fireball today!" He rubbed a sore spot on the back of his neck. "Johnny was on the other team. He convinced everyone to not hit me until Nelson blew the whistle, letting them cross the line." Tim fought back the tears. "I was hit by so many balls - I couldn't even count them!"

Bobby looked at Jamal. It was exactly the same thing that happened to him.

Tim looked up at the group and held one finger in the air. "The Power of One!" The group returned the sign of one. Everyone felt bad for Tim. Liz put her arm around her brother.

Bobby reminded everyone to be at the library on time in the morning. Everyone said goodbye and went their separate ways except Bobby, Tim, Liz, and Brad. They were going to walk home together.

The group walked out the front doors together. At the bottom of the stairs were Johnny and his thugs. "Those marks on your face kind of look like big freckles!" His buddies laughed at his comments. "You're not so mouthy right now! Was Fireball to tough for you?" Johnny and his friends laughed even harder.

Tim was about to say something really obnoxious, when Bobby stopped him. Bobby spoke to Tim quietly, "Johnny will be first on our list."

Tim looked into the eyes of Bobby. "Yep! He's first."

"Nelson is second." Bobby gritted his teeth. "It was his game. He started this."

Johnny couldn't hear what Bobby had said to Tim. "What did you say?" He moved forward a step to look intimidating.

Bobby walked down the steps and past Johnny with the others following. "I told him that you weren't worth it."

Johnny shouted back, "Come back here!"

Bobby and the others continued to walk away from him. Each of them glanced back and forth, expecting Johnny to rush up and hit them in the back.

Bobby turned around to see what had happened to Johnny. Mr. Roberts was blocking him from chasing after Bobby and the others. Bobby waited until Johnny looked at him - he held one finger pointing up. Johnny was confused as to what it could mean. Bobby turned back around to his friends. They were standing behind him with one finger pointing up as well. Bobby looked back at Johnny. He was walking the opposite way with his buddies.

Mr. Roberts stood on the steps staring at Bobby and the others. He had seen the 'Power of One' and wondered what it meant. Roberts continued to look at Bobby, and then turned around to walk back into the school. He was sure something was going on - he just hoped it was not trouble.

Bobby and the others walked a short distance without saying a word to each other. They would look quickly at Bobby's face to see his reactions. Each of them knew Johnny and his thugs were going to try to get him.

Bobby continued to walk quietly home. Finally he broke the silence, "Everything will be fine." He stopped walking and turned to the others. "Remember! We must not become like Johnny - or we are no different than him." He turned back around and continued walking home.

It was a quiet walk home. Very little was said. The group said goodbye a couple blocks from Bobby's house, and each went on their own way. They would meet in the morning at the corner and walk the rest of the way together to the city library.

Bobby walked through his old gate and up to the door. He looked around at the yard and thought, "A little paint and some repairs..."

The door opened up behind him. His mother was watching Bobby. "What are you thinking?"

"This house wouldn't be so bad if we fixed a few things and painted some others," said Bobby.

"I was thinking how pretty it would be to plant roses next spring by the fence, after it is painted and the gate repaired." His mother placed an arm around her son's shoulder.

"It could become our home." Bobby looked into his mother's eyes. It could be very beautiful again.

Bobby's mother looked down into her son's dark brown eyes. There was a change taking place in Bobby. "Yes," answered his mother. "It could become very beautiful again if given a second chance."

"Kind of like us," said Bobby. "We've been given a second chance. This is our new home."

"Do you think you can ever like it as much as our old home?" asked his mother. She was afraid how he might answer the question.

"As you always say - everything will be fine." He sounded confident. "We will be fine. I'm sure."

The two heard Bobby's father walking up the sidewalk, but something seemed strange - he was whistling - like he was happy! He opened the gate and stepped inside the yard. Bobby's father was surprised to see Bobby and his mother standing in front of the door looking at him. "What a great day!" He shouted loud enough for the neighbors to hear. "The most beautiful woman in the world awaits her husband on the front porch."

Bobby looked up at his mother's face. She stood there with a big smile on her red face. It was one of those rare times, that Bobby had ever seen her embarrassed.

He grabbed Bobby and pulled him close, while tickling him in the ribs. Bobby was so ticklish that he dropped his things to the porch and tried to get away from his father - laughing all the time.

Bobby finally got away from his dad. It had been a long time since he had seen his father like this.

"I have good news and bad news," said Bobby's father. "I've got a new job, and will start on Monday!" He became more serious. "We'll have enough money from now on to get by."

Bobby's mother began to cry. The hard times were finally going to get better.

His father wrapped his arms around her - holding her tight. "It's okay." He looked at Bobby with a big grin.

After a few minutes, Bobby's mother stepped back, "You said there was bad news?"

"We are going to have to stay in this house for some time." Bobby's father watched the reaction of his wife and son.

Bobby stepped beside his mother, " A little paint here, a little fixing there..."

"A flower here, and a flower there..." His mother looked down at Bobby. "It's our new home. Let's give it a second chance!"

Bobby and his mother laughed at each other.

"Anybody hungry?" Bobby's mother opened the door for her special guys.

"What are we having for dinner?" Bobby was really excited. It would be a great night.

"Tomatoes Ala Yuk!" answered his mother.

Bobby turned around quickly to see if his mother was serious.

She stood there grinning from ear to ear. "Gotcha!" It was a rare day to see his mother play a trick on anyone, but she had got him good. "We are having spaghetti tonight," She was very pleased to be cooking a real meal for a change. "With garlic bread."

Bobby and his father looked at each other. They couldn't remember the last time they had eaten spaghetti for dinner. They hung up their coats on the hooks, and smiled at each other.

Bobby took his school work down stairs, and turned the light on over the table. Bobby set his books and journal gently down on the table and walked over to the old worn out coat hanging on the wall. He rubbed his hand gently across its surface. Bobby would always know where he came from in life.

He sat down at the table and took out his journal. There was a lot to write about today. It was only a question of where to begin. Bobby thought about the troubles with Johnny. It didn't make sense why Johnny acted as a bully. Hurting others just didn't seem right.

Bobby started writing page after page into his journal.

It wasn't long before he heard his father's footsteps by the doorway. He turned and watched as his dad came down the stairs. Bobby could see that his father was feeling much better. He walked over to Bobby's bed and sat down. "I know it's been hard at school." His face showed a look of seriousness that Bobby had seen only a few times. "I want to hear about it all - and I mean all of it."

Bobby had never lied to his parents and wasn't going to start now. He told his father about all the conflicts with Johnny. Bobby told him about the 'Fireball' game. He could see his father's anger rising.

"I'll go to school tomorrow," said his dad.

"No," said Bobby. "This is a problem that we can solve."

"Who is we?" asked his father.

"My friends and I," answered Bobby firmly with a determined look in his eyes. "This is a problem that we can take care of."

"You don't let anyone hurt you," said his father. "And you will keep me up on everything. I don't want you in trouble."

Bobby promised his father that he would stay out of trouble. "Grandpa told me that just one person could change the world. Do you believe he is right?"

"Yes." Bobby's father looked down at his son confidently. "Do you see something wrong?"

"Yes," answered Bobby quickly.

"Then don't let it continue to happen." His father looked into Bobby's face. "But do it the right way."

"Spaghetti's on!" Bobby's mother shouted down the stairway.

Bobby's father stood up and walked over to the old coat on the wall. He placed his hand on it. "My dad wore this coat many years before he passed away. He wanted you to have it." He looked back at Bobby. "Grandpa would be very proud of you!" He smiled at Bobby. "Come on. I'm starved."

Bobby slid his chair back and started up the stairs just in front of his father. He thought, "What a great day!"

CHAPTER 7

The Committee

Bobby had a great night's sleep. He was up early and dressed. Bobby walked into the living room, sat down on the couch with a bowl of breakfast food, and started watching cartoons. His mother was sitting in the chair reading a book.

"Your father is still sleeping," said his mother over the top of the book. "Let's keep the noise down."

"What are you reading?" Bobby looked at the cover of the book.

"It's a mystery," said his mother. She turned the cover of the book toward Bobby so he could see it.

"Do want me to get you a book at the city library?" asked Bobby.

"No thanks," answered his mother. "Maybe next time."

Bobby turned the sound down on the television. He knew it was his dad's first chance in a long time to sleep in. Bobby would be very careful not to awaken him.

His mother whispered, "Your father told me about the bully at school."

Bobby looked down at his bowl of cereal.

"Why didn't you tell me?" She looked at Bobby sternly. "I don't like what I heard."

"Dad and you have enough problems to deal with." Bobby played in his cereal bowl with the spoon. "I can deal with this problem."

"Are you sure?" His mother's worries were easily seen on her face. "Is this the best way to deal with them? You know what I think of violence!"

"Mom, there will not be any violence," said Bobby in a whisper. "Everything will be alright."

Bobby's mother knew those were her exact words that she had said many times in difficult situations. She decided not to say anything more, even though she was angry with Johnny.

She placed her book down, walked over to Bobby on the couch, and sat down to watch cartoons with him. The cartoons were hard to see, but they did the best they could. Every once in awhile something would be really funny and make them laugh. They would hold their hands over their mouth trying to be quiet.

"May I join you?" Bobby's father stood there in his worn out blue jeans and an old shirt. He sat down between Bobby and his mother. His father placed an arm around each of them, and drew them closer. Soon, he was laughing hard at the cartoons on the screen.

Bobby and his mother looked at each other. It was good to see his father laughing. He looked up at the clock, "It's time for me to meet the others. It won't be long."

His father looked at him standing by the door. "Come straight home after you are finished."

"I will Dad," said Bobby, as he walked over to his coat and slipped into it. Bobby opened the door quietly, stepped outside, and closed it gently. He walked back out the front gate and turned around to look at the house. "You're not such a bad house."

Liz, Tim, and Brad were waiting for Bobby a couple of blocks away. Bobby looked at Tim to see if the red marks were still there. Most of them were gone, except one by his ear. That mark had actually bruised his skin.

"Is that bruise sore?" said Bobby, as he stared at the one by the ear.

Liz reached out and placed her finger in the center of the bruise.

"Ouch!" Tim yelped loudly.

"Yep!" Liz said between giggles. "I think it's still sore."

Tim picked up some snow and threw it at her. "Very funny!"

"What did your parents say when they saw you last night?" asked Bobby.

Liz interrupted quickly, "They thought I beat him up!" She went on, "They wanted to know what Tim had done to make me mad."

Bobby and Brad laughed. It was probably the same thing they would have thought.

"I told them what happened," said Tim quietly. "They told me to stay away from Johnny - and to control my mouth!"

"That'll be the day!" Liz was teasing her brother. "I can't imagine you controlling your mouth on any day."

Tim seemed to come to life again. "Not much chance of that is there?" He laughed with the others, as they began walking down the street together. Tim threw some more snowballs at Liz. "Mom and Dad always think it's my fault. They never blame you for anything!"

Liz placed her hands on her hips - looking Tim right in the eye. "That's because it's almost always your fault!" Liz jumped on Tim - knocking him to the ground. She pushed snow down his neck.

"I give up!" Tim stayed on the ground watching Liz, to make sure she was really going to let him up. "Well... maybe for a couple of hours!" Tim laughed at Liz and jumped to his feet.

Liz jumped right back on him, throwing snow at him from every angle. Soon, both of them were laughing and rolling in the snow. It was easy to see how close they were as twins.

Bobby and Brad helped the two up and started walking down the street again - only this time - they walked between the twins!

"My parents wanted to know what was going on at school," said Bobby as they walked.

Brad turned to Bobby. "What did you do?"

"I told them the truth," answered Bobby. "They were really angry about Johnny. My dad wanted to go to school Monday morning and talk to the principal. I convinced him to let us deal with the problem."

"Your parents are pretty cool," said Tim. "Not like mine, who let 'Miss Perfect' here get away with everything!"

Liz looked across at Tim with her eyes squinted and her lips tight together.

Tim could see she was about to attack him again. "But... I usually deserve it!" Tim grinned at Liz.

The rest of the walk, Tim continued to tease Liz. Bobby wondered if this went on all the time at home.

The group reached the city library after about forty minutes of walking, talking, and Liz trying to pound on Tim. Bobby stood for a moment at the bottom of the library's stone stairway. He could see that the library was very old. The outside of the building was built with large granite boulders. Each block was the size of Bobby. One of the blocks by the stairway had the year '1912' on it. He looked at the stone stairway going upward between four gigantic pillars. Bobby and the others began walking up the steps.

They soon reached the top of the stairs. Two large glassed front doors stood behind the pillars in front of them.

Bobby pulled back the huge doors for the others to walk in first, and then he followed them inside. The building was two stories high. A person could stand in the center of the room and see most of the second floor.

The librarians worked at a counter near the front doors. There must have been at least three or four librarians working at the same time.

Bobby and the others looked around for the rest of the group, but couldn't see them.

A lady at the counter looked up. "Are you looking for some other students working on a school project?"

"Uh…" Bobby hesitated for a moment, "Yes."

"They are in Conference Room A on the second floor." The librarian walked Bobby and the others to the center of the room. She pointed to three glassed in rooms along the wall of the second floor.

Jamal was standing by the glass wall waving down at them.

"Thank you," said Bobby to the librarian.

"You're welcome,." The librarian returned to the counter by the doors.

Bobby and the others walked up the stairs to the second floor. He looked down on the library below. Bobby thought, "I've never seen a library this big! There must be thousands of books in here."

Liz pulled on Bobby's arm. They followed Tim and Brad into the conference room and closed the door behind them. It was a small room with one long table, four chairs on each side, and one chair on each end. Maria and Stephanie were seated at the far end of the table. Each person sat down in a chair and looked around at each other. No one said a thing.

"Thanks for coming!" Bobby spoke first, "Who are we?"

"Bobby," said Tim without thinking. "We all know each other."

Liz elbowed Tim in the side. "That's not what he meant."

"Oh," answered Tim.

"I'm here because of Johnny!" Brad showed some of the anger deep inside of him. "He hurt me and got me into trouble."

"It's not just about Johnny," said Maria. "It's about all kids and even adults that hurt others." Her eyes looked down in embarrassment. "Even when they don't really realize what they are doing is hurting others." Maria looked back up into the faces of the group. She could see that they had all forgiven her for the past. A smile grew on her face, as Stephanie gave her a hug from the side.

"We are the ones who will bring bullying to an end!" said Jamal proudly. "We are the Sons and Daughters of Liberty!"

Bobby held up one finger, 'The Power of One', in front of him. The others followed by raising their finger. He looked at each person of the Committee. "The Committee has made its decision - we will be known as the Sons and Daughters of Liberty - the SDL!"

The Committee was ready for the next important decision. Each of them looked at Bobby.

"We need to design the structure of the SDL," said Bobby. He looked each member of the Committee in the face. "All decisions will be made by the Committee. The majority will rule."

"Will the Committee get any bigger?" asked Stephanie.

"No," answered Jamal quickly. "I was reading about the original Sons of Liberty during the

Revolutionary War. They had to protect their leaders from the British, so no one could know the identity of their leaders. Otherwise, the British would have caught the leaders and stopped the revolution. We must do the same."

"So," said Liz in deep thought, "No one can know who our leaders are." She thought some more. "How do we get more people to be a member of SDL?"

"Each person that joins us will only know one person." stated Jamal.

"I'm confused," said most of the Committee together at the same time.

"We will only recruit people to join us one at a time." answered Jamal. "That person will only know the person that recruited them. If I bring on five people, each person will only know me and not the others." Jamal sat back in his chair thinking about the possibilities. "There seven of us in the Committee. If each of us recruited five people, the Sons and Daughters of Liberty will be thirty five." Jamal was calculating in his mind, as fast as he could. "...And if each of those people search for five people, then the Sons and Daughters of Liberty will be one hundred and seventy five! And if each of those people recruited five people..."

"The entire school will be a part of SDL and ready to stop all the bullies forever!" Tim spoke confidently. "Then we must do it! Each of us must find our five people as soon as possible."

"What else do we need to do?" asked Brad. "We have to think of a plan to get others to join us."

"We need to start our own underground newspaper." said Bobby. "Everyone has to have the opportunity to hear our words."

"What is an underground newspaper?" asked Brad. "I've never heard of it."

"It means no one will know where the newspaper comes from or who its writers are," said Bobby. "Only the Committee will know."

"What are we going to call our newspaper?" asked Stephanie.

"Libertas!" answered Bobby quickly. "It was Jamal's idea." He smiled at Jamal. "It means liberty."

Jamal went on, "At the top of our page will be our flag - red stripes on a blue background with 'SDL' in the corner."

"The Sons and Daughters of Liberty!" said Liz with pride. "We will stand up for those students being treated wrongly!"

"Where are we going to get access to a computer and printer?" asked Brad.

"We can use my computer at home." Maria looked at the rest of the group. "It's a high quality computer and printer. My parents keep me stocked up in paper and printer cartridges."

"I can help you Maria." volunteered Jamal. "I don't live far from you."

"Great," replied Maria. "Can you come over this afternoon?"

"Sure," answered Jamal.

"How are we going to get the newsletters to the students without giving up our identity?" asked Stephanie. "We will have to be very careful."

"We will place them on mirrors in bathrooms when no one is around," said Brad.

"We can casually leave one on tables in the library and the cafeteria," added Maria.

"We could post one on the bulletin board by the office where the week's events are posted." said Liz.

Soon, everyone in the group was thinking of places to either leave the newspaper or post it on walls. Each person in the Committee took an assigned place for a copy of the 'Libertas' to be posted. They would get them out for students to see by lunch.

"Our first newsletter needs to be like the Declaration of Independence," said Jamal. "I think Bobby should write it." Each person on the Committee agreed.

Bobby accepted the job. "I am going to find a book with the Declaration of Independence in it. We can use it as a model." He stood up, walked downstairs, and went to the librarian. Bobby and the librarian walked across the room to some giant wooden bookshelves. After a short time, Bobby returned upstairs to the conference room with an old book.

"Will one of you write down what I say?" Bobby looked at the group.

"I'll do it!" answered Stephanie. She took out a notebook and pen, and waited for Bobby to say something.

"Thanks." Bobby stared at the book with the Declaration of Independence in it for a few moments, and then he looked up at the ceiling before speaking. "Many things have taken place in our school, and that takes away the dignity and respect of the students. We must speak out against those things that are wrong and expect change to take place. We believe each student is equal and should be treated as such by students and adults alike. We believe all students should be able to attend school each day without fear that someone might hurt them with either words or their body. Most of all, we believe all students have the right to be happy and safe!" He stopped for a moment to think of just the right ending. He looked at Stephanie to see if she was caught up, and back down at the book in his hands. "Therefore, we declare that bully behaviors will no longer be acceptable in our school and pledge our commitment to bring meanness to an end." Bobby took a deep breath. "Signed - The Sons and Daughters of Liberty."

The Committee sat in disbelief in their chairs. They continued staring at Bobby - they couldn't believe what they had just heard. Jamal raised one finger in front of him. Each member of the Committee did the same. It was an incredible piece of writing. Bobby turned red from embarrassment.

"We will meet Monday morning in small groups to get our first newsletter out," said Jamal. He took the time to work out the details for each member of the Committee to get their copies of the 'Libertas'. "Be very careful. Make sure no one sees you with it."

"Remember!" reminded Liz emphatically. "Everyone has to get their copies of the newsletter on the walls, mirrors, or tables before lunch."

"That takes care of the 'Libertas'," said Bobby with a smile. Everyone liked hearing its name. "What else do we need to do?"

"We have a new problem." Brad looked at each person. "Johnny told me he was going to run for Student Council President."

"Oh no!" said Tim immediately. "He'll be able to get away with even more."

"We can not let this happen!" Jamal said loudly. "One of us has to run against him." Jamal and the others looked down the table at Bobby. "It has to be you!"

"No," said Bobby emphatically. "No one knows me. I could never win."

"That's exactly what we want Johnny to believe," answered Jamal.

"Jamal is right." Maria nodded her head in agreement. "It has to be you. Johnny will never believe you can beat him, and nobody would ever dare run against him."

Brad nodded his head. "They are afraid he'll hurt them."

"Bobby?" Jamal and the others watched his face. "We need you."

"Okay." Bobby brought up his closed fist in front of him, and slowly unfolded one finger pointing up. The others quickly joined him. "It will take all of us to do this."

"What's next?" asked Tim. "I'm starved! Ouch!" He quickly received an elbow from Liz beside him.

"Now!" said Jamal. "What about Mr. Nelson?"

"What can we do about adults?" Stephanie spoke cautiously.

"Here's what we are going to do..." Bobby shared a plan to deal with Nelson. The group listened very carefully. They would giggle every once in awhile. After about ten minutes, the Committee pushed back their chairs and stood up. It was time to end the meeting. Everyone knew what to do.

Bobby reminded the group that becoming a bully was not acceptable. The Committee picked up their things and walked out of the conference room together.

Jamal stopped at the check out counter. "Could we use the conference room next Saturday?"

The lady pulled out a notebook to look at the schedule. "No problem. It's empty for at least a month. What do I call you kids?"

"The Committee!" said Bobby. Everyone in the group smiled as they each went their own ways.

"I'm starved!" This time Tim moved away from Liz so he couldn't be hit.

"Let's go to the 'BeeBop' for a pop and hotdog," said Brad. "My dad said he was proud of us and wanted to give us a treat."

"Let's go!" said Tim. "I'm starved."

Bobby and the others laughed and followed Tim down the street toward 'BeeBop's'.

About three blocks away was a small restaurant designed to look like a restaurant out of the fifty's. The group sat down at a large round booth. The cover of the seats in the booths was bright shiny red. The floor was made with black and white tiles. Everything was colored in shiny black, red, or white.

The music playing was songs from the fifties.

"What can I do for you?" a young waitress stood in front of the kids with a pencil and note pad. She wore a pink blouse with a black skirt. Bobby noticed a picture of a dog sewn in the skirt. The girl's hair was pulled back in a ponytail tied by a white scarf.

"We'd each like a pop and hotdog," answered Brad. "We'll share a large order of curly fries."

"Do you want BeeBop Goop with your fries?" asked the waitress.

Brad looked at the Liz, Tim, and Bobby. "Yes! Lots of Goop!" Each of them told the girl what they wanted to drink.

Bobby looked around the restaurant. "They never had anything like this back home!"

A group of high school girls walked in together. They sat down at the booth across from Brad and the others. "Hey!" shouted one of the girls. "Let's dance!" The girls were laughing and having a great time dancing a fifty's style dance. One of the older girls walked over to Bobby with a big smile on her face. "Come on and dance with me!"

Bobby's heart fell to the floor. "I don't know how to dance."

"Come on," said the girl, as she grabbed Bobby's hand and pulled him from the booth. "I'll show you."

It wasn't long before Bobby was learning to swing dance. He looked over at the others and laughed on one of his spins. Pretty soon, the rest of the older girls got Brad, Liz, and Tim up to dance as well.

Tim was actually great at dancing swing. He quickly learned how to do spins and twists. All of them were having a great time.

The waitress brought the hotdogs, pop, and curly fries for Bobby and the others. They thanked the older girls for teaching them how to dance, and sat back down at the booth to their food.

"That was great!" said Tim, as he bit into his hotdog. Each of them agreed that it was a lot of fun to dance fifty's style.

They finished their food and walked out the doors of the 'BeeBop', waving back at the older girls as they left.

Bobby, Liz, Tim, and Brad started walking down the street together.

"What are we going to do now?" said Liz. "There's got to be something fun to do." Liz looked at Tim with that devilish grin. "Otherwise, I'll just have to go home and beat up on my brother." She placed her arm on his shoulder and laughed.

"Let's go play 'Basement Tag' at Bobby's." Tim looked at Bobby and Brad with a big grin on his face.

"Tag?" questioned Liz. "Isn't that kind of ... childish?"

"I think it might make your standards," said Tim. "We'll even let you be 'it' first!"

Liz knew something was up just by the grins on the boys' faces. She thought, "They're going to try and get me, but I'll get them first!" Liz smiled as they walked to Bobby's house. "Boys always think they're smarter...not!"

The group walked through the old gate at Bobby's house and up to the porch. Tim looked at Bobby with a sly grin, "This will be fun."

Bobby opened the door to his house for Liz, Brad, and Tim to enter. Bobby's parents were sitting on the couch talking to each other.

"Hi Mrs. T!" said Tim. "Good to see you again Mr. T."

"Good to see you, Tim." Bobby's father stood up to greet each of the kids.

"I'm Liz. Unfortunately, Tim is my brother." Liz gave Tim an elbow in the ribs. "We're twins."

"Twins!" Bobby's father smiled at Liz. He thought, "I'm sure you can hold your own with Tim."

"I'm Brad," he showed some of his shyness. "Hi Mrs. T!"

"I'm glad to meet you Brad." Bobby's father made sure Brad felt comfortable.

Bobby's mother smiled back at Brad and the others. "Hi kids. Are you hungry?"

Bobby told his parents about the nice treat at the 'BeeBop', and how the older girls tried to teach them a fifty's dance. Brad, Liz, and Tim added their versions of the experience.

"Do you mind if we play 'Basement Tag' for a while?" asked Bobby. "We'll be careful."

Bobby's parents looked at each other and grinned. "Sure," said his mother. "I'll have some hot chocolate in about an hour."

"Great," said Tim. "I'll need some hot chocolate after I get these guys."

Bobby led Liz, Brad, and Tim downstairs. Brad explained the rules of the game to Liz. She had that smile on her face, which could only mean trouble for the boys.

Upstairs, Bobby's parents looked at each other. "I'm betting on Liz," said Bobby's mother. She took out some knitting and started making another scarf.

"I think your right,' answered Bobby's father. He picked up a magazine and began to read it.

Liz was 'it' first. Bobby noticed a look of trickery in her eyes. He was sure that Liz would make the game even more exciting.

Bobby, Brad, and Tim spread out in the room away from Liz, while she held the switch to the light with her fingers. Liz looked at each boy with a twinkle in her eyes, "Your mine!" Liz turned off the light.

Bobby, Brad, and Tim each scattered in different directions - then stopped moving. They were trying to hear Liz moving around on the floor. There was no sound anywhere. She was far quieter at the game than them. Bobby moved to a corner, pulled his knees up tight to his chest, and tried to listen for sounds.

Brad moved over beside the bed, and worked his body between the table and the bed. He was sure that Liz would have a hard time finding him there.

Tim was sitting in the middle of the floor. He figured Liz would work the edges of the room looking for him and the other boys. He listened carefully - but heard nothing. Tim waited for a long time - there was no sound! "Come on Liz!" yelled Tim. "You have to look for us."

Tim never knew Liz was right behind him. She screamed in his ear and grabbed him, "You're 'it'!"

Liz scared Tim so bad, that he let out a scream! Even Bobby and Brad couldn't help but laugh. Brad found the light switch and turned on the lights. Liz was on Tim's back laughing as hard as she could. Tim was still trying to get his breath back.

Bobby's mother looked at her husband, "Liz got Tim!"

"Yep." Bobby father never looked up from his reading, even though he was smiling. "I figured that was going to happen."

Tim finally got his breath back, "You were just lucky!" He pushed Liz off his back. "We were just taking it easy on you," said Tim. He winked at Brad and Bobby. "This time the winner is determined by who is last to get caught. Each person that gets caught is 'it' as well. The last person will try to hide from the other three." Tim laughed at his sister. "We'll see how good you really are!"

Brad was confused, "If you find me in the dark, then we are both 'it'?"

"You got it!" Tim figured that he would catch Brad and Bobby first. Then, all three of them would scare Liz to death. He laughed inside just thinking how much fun it would be.

Tim placed his hand on the light switch and turned it off. There were all kinds of noises in the dark - then silence. He moved around the floor of the room. Tim was pretty sure there was a noise to his right, so he jumped at it. He hit Brad in the side. Brad had definitely been scared by the contact. Now, the two of them were hunting for Bobby and Liz.

Brad and Tim worked side by side along the edge of the bed. Brad felt the edge of a shoe in front of him. He tapped Tim on the shoulder - then both boys jumped into the darkness. Bobby was caught totally by surprise and let out a shriek.

Bobby's father looked at his wife, "I believe that shrill was your son."

She smiled back at her husband, "Sounds just like his father."

Tim had accomplished what he had wanted to do. The three boys worked the floor in search of Liz. After about thirty minutes of searching, they finally gave up. Bobby turned on the light. There was no sign of Liz anywhere. They looked under the bed and behind everything.

Bobby was beginning to worry and decided to walk upstairs to tell his parents what had happened. "Have you guys seen Liz?" Bobby's eyes saw the unbelievable.

At the kitchen table having hot chocolate with both his parents was Liz! She sat there with a big grin on her face as Brad and Tim finally joined Bobby.

Liz told Bobby's parents how much fun the game was, but never said a word on how she got up the stairs without the boys knowing. Liz was truly the champion of 'Basement Tag'! Bobby, Tim, and Brad joined the others at the table for hot chocolate. Tim tried to convince everyone that he let Liz catch him the first time, but they knew different.

After a short time, Brad, Liz, and Tim left for their homes. Bobby stood on the front porch and watched them as they walked down the street. He thought, "It's great to have friends again!"

CHAPTER 8

Libertas

On Monday morning each person of the Committee came to school early and walked by Jamal and Maria at the front doors of the school. They talked for a moment while Maria and Jamal quickly slipped copies of the 'Libertas' inside their coats. After a few moments, each member of the Committee smiled and disappeared into the crowded hallways of the school. Jamal gave Stephanie an extra piece of paper and smiled.

Jamal looked at Maria across from him - no one had seen them handing out copies of the newspaper to the Committee. He had to hurry. Jamal had a couple of important things to do before meeting Bobby at the office. He winked at Maria, then turned around and walked quickly down the hallway toward the gym.

Bobby stood in front of the office watching the clock and waiting for Jamal to get there. He saw Jamal coming toward him. "Did you have any problems?"

"None." Jamal gave Bobby a big smile. "It's all done." He turned to walk into the office. "Come on. We have to hurry!"

The two boys opened the glass doors and walked into the busy office. Several students were sitting in chairs or waiting at the counter. One student was on the phone talking to their parent.

Jamal got the attention of the secretary, "Bobby wants to run for Student Council President. Is there a form he needs to fill out?"

Actually," said the secretary abruptly, "The two people you need to talk are walking in right behind you."

Jamal and Bobby turned around as Mr. Reed and Mr. Roberts walked into the office together with a copy of the 'Libertas' in their hands. Jamal and Bobby gave a quick glance at each other.

The secretary waited for Mr. Roberts to look her direction, and then she pointed her hand at Jamal and Bobby.

Mr. Roberts must have understood her sign language. "What's happening guys?"

Jamal spoke up for Bobby, "He wants to run for Student Council President." Jamal tried to look very serious. "Does he need to fill out any forms?"

Mr. Roberts looked at Bobby. "Are you sure that you want to do this?"

"Yes sir," answered Bobby. "I want to run for President."

"You will be running against Johnny," said Mr. Roberts. "Do you want to change your mind?"

"No sir," answered Bobby quickly. "This is something I really want to do."

"Good!" Mr. Roberts finally smiled at Bobby. "Here is a form that your parents must sign. You bring it back to me tomorrow." Mr. Roberts glanced at Mr. Reed, who was reading a copy of the 'Libertas' carefully.

"This writing looks very familiar!" Reed was lost in thought. "I have seen this style of writing before."

"Bobby's going to run for President," said Mr. Roberts to Mr. Reed.

"Great!" Mr. Reed looked genuinely pleased for Bobby. "I'm proud of you."

"Here are the rules for the campaign and the election. The campaign begins tomorrow. It will last for two weeks. One week from this Friday is an assembly. Johnny and you will give speeches to the entire school, followed by an all school election." Roberts started to hand the papers to Bobby, but Jamal took them first.

"I'm his campaign manager," said Jamal. "I'll make sure he follows the rules completely."

"Good luck!" Roberts shook Bobby's hand then turned back to Mr. Reed, who was still reading the newspaper. "What do you make of it?"

Mr. Reed was staring at the 'Libertas'. "The writing looks so familiar to me. I just can't place it."

Jamal and Bobby looked at each other, as the two teachers walked out of the office. "Do you think Reed will figure it out?" asked Jamal.

"I don't know," replied Bobby. "He's seen my writing a couple of times, and..."

"And what?" asked Jamal.

"He read some of my journal last week." Bobby looked concerned. "He complimented my writing style."

"Let's hope he doesn't figure it out." Jamal was grinning. "Look at the counter in front of the secretary's desk."

Bobby had to chuckle. Jamal had taped a copy of the 'Libertas' on the front side of the counter facing students. Already, a couple of students were reading it.

Bobby and Jamal left the office quickly. Neither one wanted to be late for classes and draw attention to themselves. Bobby started noticing copies of the 'Libertas' everywhere. The Committee had completed the first stage of the plan.

Bobby entered the classroom almost at the very same time as the bell rang. Mr. Reed was still looking at a copy of the newspaper, and never noticed Bobby walking in.

Everyone was in his or her seats including Johnny. Bobby glanced at him out the corner of his eye, but tried to ignore him.

Stephanie smiled as Bobby walked down the outside row toward his seat. Her smile told him that she had completed her assigned tasks. Bobby placed his things on the desk and looked at Brad. He was smiling also - his tasks were completed! Bobby glanced at Tim. His huge grin told Bobby that he had completed his tasks as well.

"Good!" Bobby thought. "Everything is going according to the plan." He glanced at the bulletin board on the side of the room - a copy of 'Libertas' was posted for all to see.

Mr. Reed sat down on an empty desk in the front of the room. "First, I'd like to make an important announcement." Mr. Reed held a copy of the 'Libertas' in his hands. "Student Council elections for President are in two weeks. Today was the final day for candidates to declare their intention to run."

Johnny sat at his desk all puffed up. He was sure no one had run against him. He would be president without having to do anything.

"There will be two candidates for you to choose from," said Mr. Reed casually.

Johnny nearly fell out of his chair. What kid would dare run against him? His face turned red as the anger began to grow inside him.

"And both candidates are in this room right now!" exclaimed the teacher.

It was as if the air left the room. Each student looked at the other. Johnny searched the room, trying to figure out who it was.

"Congratulations to Johnny," Mr. Reed hesitated, "And Bobby!"

Every student looked back at Bobby in horror. What would make him think of crossing Johnny?

"Let's give both of these boys a hand." Mr. Reed led the class in a clapping of the hands for both boys. "Congratulations to you both."

Bobby hadn't expected this in the plan. The word would travel like wildfire through the classrooms.

Maria seated across from Johnny leaned close to him, "Don't worry! Nobody knows him."

Johnny looked back at her, "Of course! He's a nobody!"

Maria looked back at Bobby and smiled.

He thought, "Nice work Maria! Johnny took the bait, hook, line, and sinker!"

Maria stared at Bobby and rubbed her eye casually with one finger - the Power of One! Bobby did the same.

Mr. Reed held up a copy of the 'Libertas' in front of his face. "This morning, copies of this newsletter appeared all over the school. How many of you have already seen this?"

Hands slowly began to rise into the air. Bobby was surprised to see that almost every student in the room had read the newspaper already. Johnny was one of the few that had not seen it.

"We are going to discuss the content of this newsletter called..." Mr. Reed turned the letter around to read the title. "The 'Libertas'!" He stared at the newspaper for a moment then read the entire page to the class. "Let's begin by analyzing what it means. The title 'Libertas' is Latin for liberty. Latin is a very old language used by the Romans a couple thousand years ago.

Mr. Reed began to read the writing slowly to the class. "Many things have taken place in our school, which take away the dignity and respect of students." He stopped for a moment. "What do you think this writer meant?"

Bobby got the attention of Maria, Brad, and Tim not to answer any questions. Their answers would be a sure give away.

"I think the person who wrote this was picked on by some one." Mary looked at Mr. Reed seriously. "He or she is tired of bullies!"

"Do we have people in our school like this?" asked the teacher.

"Yes!" said Mary. "I'm tired of it, and so are a lot of other students."

Bobby was impressed with Mary's direct answer. Maria looked back at Bobby and nodded her head. Mary would be her first recruit.

Mr. Reed called on Doug, who raised his hand at the back of the room by the window.

"There has been too many times someone has tried to hurt someone," said Doug. "You know - like bumping into them and telling them it was an accident. Then when they get caught, the bully always says, 'I was just kidding'! The bully isn't kidding - they are being mean." Doug tried not to look toward Johnny.

Brad glanced at Bobby. Doug would be his recruit.

Mr. Reed read some more from the 'Libertas'. "We must speak out against those things that are wrong and expect change to take place." He looked up from the newspaper and called on a girl with her hand up at the front of the room.

"We can't be afraid to speak out against those who hurt us! We need to help each other," stated Sarah emphatically.

Bobby listened to student after student, explaining what they thought the 'Libertas' meant. Bobby knew many of these students would make great SDL members. He was pleased that the students understood the meaning of his writing.

Mr. Reed talked to the students for a moment, "The writer tells us three major things about his or her beliefs. Here's what was said in the newspaper." Mr. Reed looked into the faces of the students. "We believe each student is equal and should be treated as such by students and adults alike. We believe all students should be able to attend school each day without fear that someone might hurt them with either words or their body. Most of all, we believe all students have the right to be happy and safe!"

"The writer of this newspaper has said what each of us believes," said a quiet voice from the back of the room. It was Thomas, a very small shy boy. "This is exactly what we would say if we were brave enough."

Mr. Reed looked at Thomas and thanked him for his answer. Bobby knew that he would talk to Thomas personally.

Mr. Reed read the rest of the 'Libertas' to the class. "Therefore, we declare that bully behaviors will no longer be acceptable at our school and pledge our commitment to bring meanness to an end. Signed - The Sons and Daughters of Liberty." Mr. Reed looked at the class. "What do you think this means?"

"I think war has begun," said Johnny. No one laughed at his comment.

"I don't think it is about war!" Bobby looked at Johnny. "It's about not being a victim any longer and standing together for what is right." Bobby continued to stare at Johnny. Some students were thinking Bobby was crazy for making Johnny angry again.

Others agreed with Bobby and shared their point of view. Bobby listened as student after student began to share their opinions and experiences of dealing with a bully.

The bell rang ending the discussion. Most students believed it was the best class of the year.

Bobby walked out of the class with one eye on Johnny and the other on Mr. Reed. The teacher was still staring at the paper trying to remember why it was so familiar.

Johnny watched Bobby as he left the room. He thought, "Little jerk! I'll get you later."

"It's a good thing you didn't touch Bobby," said Maria to Johnny.

"Why is that?" replied Johnny.

"If you pick on him, then everyone will feel bad for Bobby and elect him president," answered Maria. "It's better to keep him a nobody." Maria saw a couple of girls she wanted to recruit. "Hey guys! Wait for me."

Johnny thought about what Maria had just said to him. It made perfect sense.

Maria looked back at Johnny as she walked out. Bobby was waiting just outside the door for her. "He bought it!" She smiled at Bobby and continued to walk with the girls down the hallway. Bobby was sure she was recruiting.

"Thomas," Bobby spoke softly in the hallway. "Can I walk with you?"

Thomas looked at him cautiously, "Sure."

"You've been picked on by someone haven't you?" Bobby's caring eyes made Thomas feel secure.

"Johnny and his buddies threw me in the trash can behind the school yesterday and took my lunch money." Thomas was near tears.

"You come and set with me in the cafeteria. I'll share my lunch with you." Bobby smiled at Thomas. "Everything will be fine." Bobby continued to walk with Thomas down the hallway. Thomas was sure to be a member of the SDL.

Thomas stopped walking, "You are one of the Sons and Daughters of Liberty - aren't you?"

Bobby stared at Thomas. "Yes. We want you to join us!"

Thomas told Bobby that he was excited to stop bullies like Johnny and knew a couple more friends just like him. The two said goodbye and parted. Bobby knew the SDL was growing larger with each passing minute.

Bobby hurried to gym class for a whole new game of Fireball. He walked through the giant doors and went straight for the shoebox. Bobby dug through the old shoes until he found the ones he wore at the last class, placed them in his hands, and walked over to the bench. He sat down by Jamal, who was grinning from ear to ear.

"Have you seen Nelson yet?" asked Bobby as he tied his shoes.

"Nope," answered Jamal with a chuckle. "He must be having a problem." The two looked at each other and laughed.

Nelson had a problem indeed. He always used two lockers side by side to get dressed for class. The locker next to his workout clothes was open. He undressed quickly and placed all of his clothes in the locker. Nelson reached for the door of the locker and slammed it shut. There was note attached to the front of the door. It was a copy of the 'Libertas'. Someone had circled the word 'adult' on it.

The gym teacher reached for his locker door to open it. The door was jammed and couldn't be opened. He tried over and over to open it, but failed. Nelson looked up at the clock. He was already late for class.

Nelson decided put on his dress clothes again for class and get the locker door fixed. He tried to open the door to his dress clothes, but it was jammed as well. The teacher had no clothes to wear and couldn't open either locker. Nelson pounded on the locker door with his fists a couple of times. He looked up at the clock again. All of his clothes were locked up in the jammed lockers! What was he going to wear?

Nelson glanced back at the clock again. He was really late. No one was with the students. The teacher saw some used clothes in a box by the door. There was no choice; he would have to find something in the box that would fit him. He looked down into the small pile of clothes. There were only a few pieces inside. Most were too small for the teacher. Mr. Nelson's eyes saw only one pair that would fit him. His stomach turned upside down as he looked down at them. He lifted the clothes out of the box. A copy of the 'Libertas' fell out of the shirt. The teacher watched the paper float slowly to the floor. He glanced back at the clock and back at the clothes in his hands. Nelson had to hurry; he could get into trouble for not being with the students.

Jamal looked at the clock and then at Bobby, "We should be having a guest just about now." They both watched the gym doors open right on cue.

Ms. Stewart, the principal walked into the gym class through the doors at that moment and looked around the room for the teacher. The principal couldn't see Mr. Nelson anywhere. Stewart was popular with the students. The kids knew she was strict, but always fair.

Jamal and Bobby slapped each others hands in front of them. "Right on schedule!" said Jamal calmly. "She must have seen the note on her door."

"What did the note say?" said Bobby with a couple of giggles.

"The Sons and Daughters of Liberty believe Mr. Nelson's treatment of students can no longer be allowed. It is time for him to change," answered Jamal.

Stewart asked several of the students where Mr. Nelson was. No one seemed to know. "Alright you guys," said Ms. Stewart. "Let's do warm ups. Get into the lines you were in last class."

Everyone quickly hurried to his place. Even the kids in line five remembered this time. Exercises were completely different. There was no whistle or threatening voice. Everyone seemed to enjoy it and tried hard.

They were almost done when the locker room door opened slowly. Mr. Nelson peered out the door with his head only. He saw the principal teaching his class. The gym teacher knew there was no choice, except to walk out into the room.

Jamal got Bobby's attention. Mr. Nelson moved slowly to the front of the gym and Ms. Stewart. He was trying not to get the attention of the class, but it didn't work.

Everyone stopped exercising and stared at Nelson in silence as the two adults talked. They had never seen anything like it before. Mr. Nelson was dressed in shorts that were a bright pink and a yellow shirt with a leopard skin look. His socks were ugly green!

Nelson held two copies of the 'Libertas' in his hand. He pointed to the circled word 'adult'. "I want these people caught!"

The principal's eyes continued to look at the clothes Nelson was wearing as he spoke. It wasn't long before the principal showed the teacher the note.

"I can't teach in these clothes," answered Nelson in a loud voice to the principal. Every student in the gym could hear him.

"There are no substitutes," said Ms. Stewart. "Sorry. You have to make do until I can get the doors to the locker opened." The principal turned and walked away from Mr. Nelson. She glanced at the faces of the students in the room. She thought, "I'd say that was a pretty clear message Mr. Nelson - I hope you were listening."

Nelson finished the exercise. There was no whistle - it was inside the jammed locker. The students tried not to stare at the unusually dressed teacher, but it was very hard not to do! This was a whole new fashion statement.

Mr. Nelson just didn't seem to have his usual enthusiasm during class. "Let's play Fireball. Even number lines down there, and odd numbered lines at this end." He picked up the ball bag and dumped it out. Nothing but yellow nerf balls rolled out onto the floor. A copy of the 'Libertas' floated to the floor. Nelson's eyes watched helplessly as the newspaper lay face up. He saw the word 'adult' circled on it. The gym teacher was beginning to get the message.

The students picked up the nerf balls and started to throw them at each other immediately. Nobody was going to get hurt today. The laughter of the kids soon grew very loud. Everyone was enjoying the game and feeling safe.

Jamal stared at Mr. Nelson sitting on the bench looking pretty worn out. He looked back at Bobby, who was holding one finger up. The two grinned from ear to ear and went back to the game.

Jamal and Bobby walked into the lunchroom together. They saw Tim and Brad on the far side of the room, talking to a group of kids.

Tim looked up to see Bobby and Jamal grinning, then turned back to the students and continued talking. He was excited to hear Bobby and Jamal explain what Fireball was like today.

The girls were sitting back at their table watching Bobby and Jamal as well. They knew it was time for Johnny to get his! Maria left the girls and started toward the lunch line.

Johnny came wandering into the lunchroom by himself. For some strange reason, his thugs weren't with him. He looked around the room with an overconfident look. Johnny hadn't noticed that Maria was right behind him.

"Hey there," said Maria, as she stood in front of him. "Are you worried about losing the election to Bobby?"

"No way," Johnny answered even more confidently. "I can beat him without even trying."

"That's a great idea," answered Maria. "If you do nothing to campaign, then you'll win in a land side. No one will ever know who he is." Maria watched Johnny's face as he thought about it.

Johnny was bumped into from his backside fairly hard. He started to turn around, but Maria got his attention.

"You will have no problem winning." Maria continued to lead Johnny's brain down the path. "Just don't give people a reason to know who he is - leave him alone!"

Johnny kept thinking about what Maria had said. He looked at Bobby sitting down at a table with Jamal. "I can't bring attention to him - I'll just have to ignore him for now - later I will get even!"

Students everywhere were noticing Johnny. He figured it was because of the election. Johnny went through the lunch line and walked around most of the lunchroom. He sat down with a small group of students, who sat quietly listening to him. After a short time, he finished his lunch and walked out the door. He passed by Mr. Roberts in the doorway.

Roberts stared at Johnny's back as he walked by. A large note was stuck to the back of his shirt. 'Bullies Beware!' It was signed by the SDL.

Students passing by Johnny saw the note, but no one was going to tell him.

The week passed by without any great problems. Mr. Nelson eventually got the locker doors opened, but not before someone got a picture of him in his cute pink and leopard skin outfit. Pictures kept popping up around the school. Some said it was on the internet. For the most part, Nelson's classes were much better. The little red balls completely disappeared, and were never found. Some people wondered how the principal appeared at just the right moment.

Johnny was leaving Bobby alone. It was strange to watch. You could tell he wanted to attack him, but Maria's words kept reminding him not to do it. Rumor had it that Johnny never saw the note on his back - he wore it all day, until some one bumped into him again and removed it - but who could be that well organized?

The Committee continued to stay away from each other all week. No one knew how many recruits had been brought into the SDL, but the number was growing every day.

Saturday morning finally arrived. Each member of the Committee met at the city library again for the final planning of the election and the SDL. Everyone was excited to share his or her week with the group.

"Everybody is talking about SDL at school." said Liz excitedly. "The 'Libertas' was a huge success. Many kids are wondering when the next copy will be out."

"Thursday," answered Bobby. "We must do it right before the elections. It will be our call to arms!" He looked at the Committee. Everyone was in agreement. "Maria," said Bobby, "I will get you the final copy on Wednesday."

"That will work," said Maria. "Jamal and I will be by the door again waiting for all of you Thursday morning. We'll use the same method."

"How many people have we recruited into the SDL?" Tim was excited.

"I found six!" said Liz.

"I got four!" added Brad.

"I found seven!" answered Bobby.

"Nine!" added Jamal.

"Five!" answered Stephanie.

"Seven!" said Maria proudly. "Including Whitney!"

Everyone looked at Tim. "I recruited twenty-six." He said the number casually. "I'm just a good talker." The group laughed hard.

Jamal had been calculating the numbers. "Our goal was thirty five. We recruited sixty-four! Good job everyone. I wonder how many people each of them have recruited."

The group sat quietly just thinking about how the number was growing larger.

"It is time for some fun before we do the rest of our planning." Bobby looked at Maria, "How did you get the note on Johnny's back?"

"It was easy," said Maria. "While I was talking to Johnny, Liz bumped into him from behind and stuck the note on his back. At the end of the day, we just did it again, and took it back. He never knew what we were doing."

"Kids all over the school saw the note," said Liz jokingly. "No one told him anything including several teachers."

Bobby looked at Jamal, "Tell us how you dealt with Nelson. Your plan was excellent!"

"I went into the locker room before school. I had noticed on another day that he always uses the same two lockers, which made it easy. I went to the two lockers that Nelson used. He never kept them locked. I opened the one with his gym clothes, jammed the door lock, and slammed it shut. I tried to open it, but it was stuck tight. I did the same with the other locker, but left the door open. When he closed the door it jammed automatically." Jamal leaned back in his chair. "All I had to do was write a note to the principal, to get her in the gym at the perfect time."

"How did you get the note to the office without being noticed?" asked Brad.

"That was my job," answered Stephanie. "They are so used to me in the office, nobody noticed when I placed the note on Ms. Stewart's door. She always checks her messages at that time of day."

"What about the red-balls?" asked Bobby. "Where are they?"

"The balls are underneath the dirty towels in the locker room," said Jamal. "I figured it would be the last place Nelson would look for them."

The grouped clapped for Jamal. He had proven himself to be a master of stealth.

"What do we need to do next?" asked Stephanie.

The group sat quietly thinking. No one was sure what was next.

"We can not continue writing our newsletter anonymously," said Bobby quietly. "At some point in time, each of us will have to stand up publicly for our beliefs." Bobby went on, "Although it may seem like fun, what we did to Johnny and Mr. Nelson must end. Otherwise, we will likely become bullies like them. One of my classes was spent just talking about the 'Libertas'. We need to create a talk in our school that ends bully behaviors."

The Committee knew Bobby was right. They didn't look forward to the day when everyone would know it was them behind the 'Libertas'.

"I suggest we wait until the election is over on Friday," said Jamal. "We can write our last newsletter at that time and sign our real names."

The Committee looked at each other and agreed. It was the right thing to do.

"There is only one thing left to do," said Tim. "Let's go to the BeeBop and have fun!"

The Committee picked up their things and went to the restaurant only a couple blocks away. They squeezed the whole group around the biggest table in the room. Everyone order a pop. It wasn't long before the music was turned on and Tim was dancing on the floor. Bobby and the others joined him in the fun. The entire group was having a great time.

Stephanie stopped dancing in the middle of the room. She stared at the doorway to the restaurant. The eyes of the group followed hers to the door. Johnny was standing in the doorway watching them. He looked from person to person in the room until he saw Maria. His brain quickly put it all together. The redness in his neck grew brighter,

"Pretty smart," said Johnny to Maria. He walked up to Bobby and quickly pushed Bobby backward into a table. "Now, we'll see if you and your new friends are so smart." Johnny turned around and walked out of the restaurant.

"It's my fault," said Bobby to the group. "We shouldn't have all come here together." Brad helped Bobby to his feet.

"We have to be careful," said Brad. "Johnny's meanness will really come out."

"Well," said Bobby, "There is only one thing left to do." Each person expected something wise to come from Bobby's mouth. Instead, it was, "Basement Tag!"

Brad, Liz, and Tim laughed loudly. They shouted together, "Basement Tag!"

"What's Basement Tag?" said Jamal.

"Oh," said Liz. "It's just a simple tag game." Her eyes twinkled at the thought of seven playing the game in the darkness of Bobby's basement.

Tim wondered who would be the first to scream.

Bobby was thinking about Johnny. "Trouble is just around the corner!"

CHAPTER 9

Mud

Basement Tag was great with seven people. There were plenty of screams for everyone. The group broke up and went home after about an hour. Their happiness quickly disappeared. Bobby could see the look of anxiousness in each face, as they wondered what Johnny would do to them on Monday.

Bobby spent the rest of Saturday and Sunday quietly thinking about Johnny. He was sure that Johnny would be very spiteful!

Monday morning finally came. Bobby met Brad, Liz, and Tim down the street.

"Hi guys," said Bobby, trying to cover up his nervousness.

Brad didn't waste a moment getting to the point. "What do you think Johnny will do?"

"I don't know," answered Bobby. "I'm sure it will be bad!"

"There is one good thing," added Liz. "He doesn't know that we are the writers of the 'Libertas'."

"That's true." Bobby thought about it as they walked. "He only knows that our group was hanging out together." He continued to think more about the situation. "Johnny will probably get after Maria first. We'd better hurry to school and find her."

Bobby and the others walked as fast as they could. There was no sign of Maria, Stephanie, or Whitney outside the doors to the school. They walked in and looked around, then continued walking down the hallway.

"There's Stephanie and Whitney standing by the office." Liz walked over to the girls with Bobby and Brad right behind her. "Where's Maria?"

Stephanie pointed toward the office with her hand. The group looked through the glass windows to see what was going on.

Maria was standing at the counter talking to someone on the phone. She set the phone down and turned around. She was a mess of dirty water and mud spots from her head to her shoes. Maria's beautiful pink coat and dress looked ruined. Her brown hair was hanging straight down with droplets of mud mixed in it. Tears trickled from her mud-covered eyes down her cheeks and over her chin. The sadness in Maria's eyes was heart breaking, as she looked out at the group for just a brief second, and then sat down in a chair with her back to them. Her back began to quiver slightly. They were pretty sure she was crying.

"Maria was walking by herself to school this morning," said Stephanie sadly. "We were supposed to meet at the front doors."

Whitney continued the story. "Johnny hid in some bushes about a block away. He jumped out and threw a bucket of muddy water at her. She never saw it coming."

"Did he say anything?" Tim was getting angrier by the moment.

"He told her it was an accident and laughed at her," answered Stephanie. "As he walked away from her, Johnny told her that she had better not be around all of us again, and this is what she gets for trying to protect the new kid."

Bobby couldn't believe that Johnny had done such a mean thing to Maria. He was sure that all of them would find out how rotten Johnny could be. Bobby looked back in the office at Maria sitting by herself.

Stephanie and Whitney opened the door of the office and went in. Maria slowly lowered her head down into her hands, as Stephanie sat down beside her.

Bobby and the others watched as Maria lay her head on Stephanie's shoulder - they knew she was sobbing. It hurt just to watch her.

Suddenly, Brad was shoved into Liz and Tim. His books fell on the floor. They were kicked clear across the hallway!

"Oops! Sorry!" It was Johnny and his familiar words. "You have to watch where you're going 'dufus' - somebody could get hurt!" Johnny's eyes pierced Brad like an arrow. "You picked the wrong team to be on." Johnny turned back around and headed for Mr. Reed's class.

Bobby continued to watch as Johnny walked down the hallway laughing loudly. He stopped after a short distance, and looked back at Bobby watching him. Johnny mouthed the words, "You're mine!" He turned backed around and disappeared down the hallway in the mist of kids heading to class.

Bobby and the others helped Brad gather up his things. They looked at Maria in the office one more time, and headed off to class. Brad, Tim, and Bobby walked into class together.

Johnny sat in his chair watching as they walked into the room. He looked like a shark ready to attack another victim. His sly grin and piercing blue eyes watched the boys all the way to their seats.

Bobby watched him out the corner of his eye. He wanted to make sure Johnny was staying in his seat.

Brad would not look at all in Johnny's direction. The bully had placed a huge amount of fear in Brad very quickly.

Tim stared at Johnny, as he walked along the wall. "Jerk," said Tim in a whisper only loud enough for Bobby to hear.

Mr. Reed looked around the room, as he did his attendance. "Has anyone seen Maria?"

Many of the students in the room had already heard what Johnny did. They sat quietly at their seats saying nothing.

"I heard she went home," said Johnny coyly to Mr. Reed. "I guess she got a little mud on her." Johnny chuckled to himself, as he looked back over his shoulder at Bobby, Tim, and Brad. "She must have needed a change in clothes." Johnny chuckled some more to himself. "Pink and mud just aren't her colors." He laughed some more.

"Last week, we were discussing the newspaper that popped up all over the school. Does anyone have any more thoughts they would like to share?" Mr. Reed looked around the room. No hands were raised to speak. Something had changed!

The teacher hadn't noticed how many of the students looked toward Johnny and then back down at their books. There was no way the students were going to discuss bullies today.

Mr. Reed figured something was up, but would find out later. "Open your books to Page 345. I would like you to read the story and answer the questions on Page 356. We will go over your answers tomorrow in class." Mr. Reed spent the rest of class walking around the room, looking over the shoulders of the students. He stopped by a copy of the 'Libertas' on the wall, and thought, "Will there be a second 'Libertas'?"

The class ended quietly. Johnny was one the first out the door, and disappeared quickly down the hallway.

Bobby, Brad, and Tim looked seriously at each other. "We've got to be very careful," said Bobby in a cautious voice. "Johnny's not going to stop!"

The three boys broke up and went their separate ways. Tim looked around for Johnny, but couldn't see the bully anywhere. Tim decided to make a quick stop at the bathroom. As he walked into the door, Tim was grabbed by his coat and pulled inside. "You jerk!" The words flew from Tim's mouth in a second. He was quickly pushed to the floor. Two sets of hands pinned Tim down to the floor, so that he couldn't move.

"My mom always said the best way to clean up a bad mouth is with soap!" Johnny took a handful of soap and shoved it in Tim's mouth. Johnny looked down at Tim with a vicious look. "How does that feel Mr. Mouth?" Johnny and his buddies let loose of Tim and walked out of the bathroom laughing.

Tim quickly got back up on his feet and began spitting out the soap. His usual cocky look was gone, Tim was truly afraid. He gathered his things quickly and got out of the bathroom. Tim stepped into the hallway - looked both directions for Johnny and his thugs, and then began walking slowly in the direction of his class. He had never been this afraid before.

The group met at the back table for lunch. The whole group except Maria sat down quietly.

"Where's Maria?" asked Bobby.

"She went home," said Stephanie. "She told her mother that she was sick."

"Did she tell her mom what happened?" asked Bobby.

"No," said Stephanie quickly. "She's afraid of Johnny and his buddies." Stephanie waited for a second, and then spoke up. "I hear someone else told Mr. Roberts and Ms. Stewart about it." Stephanie winked at the group.

Each person sat quietly thinking about Maria, and what she had looked like. They wondered who would be next.

Liz looked at her brother questioningly, "You're quiet." Her eyes watched him very closely.

"I'm just thinking." Tim never said a word about the bathroom incident, but it was clearly on his mind.

"I wish you would do more of that 'thinking' stuff at home." Liz was trying to get a little humor back into the group. Usually, Tim could get everyone to laugh. Liz's eyes looked past the group.

Johnny walked into the cafeteria with his buddies. He was clearly enjoying the power over Bobby and the others. Johnny sat down at a table nearby. His steely blue eyes purposefully stared at each member of the group one by one.

Bobby and the others never said a word to each other. Johnny's intimidation was clearly working. Students everywhere in the cafeteria were watching the results.

"Let's go to the library," said Stephanie. She said it loud enough for everyone and including Johnny to hear. The group picked up their trays and left the table.

Bobby looked back. Johnny and his buddies were right behind them.

"Lets stay right beside them no matter where they go," said Johnny loudly to his buddies. "Watch them squirm!"

Ms. Stewart and Mr. Roberts stepped right in front of Johnny. "Are you finished eating?" said the principal.

"Yes, Ms. Stewart." Johnny's politeness was almost sickening. "Is there something wrong?"

Mr. Roberts took Johnny's tray out of his hands, and handed it to one of his buddies. "Would you please put this up for Johnny?"

"Sure thing!" said the boy nervously. "No problem!"

"Oh boys!" Mr. Roberts walked back over to Johnny's buddies. "It seems to me, that you are both making some very bad decisions lately." Roberts turned back around and left with Johnny and the principal.

The boy with Johnny's tray looked nervously at the other. "I'm not going to hang out with Johnny anymore. Roberts knows something." The other boy nodded is head.

Johnny walked into the Principal's Office with Ms. Stewart and Mr. Roberts. He sat down in a chair straight across from Ms. Stewart. Mr. Roberts remained standing and leaning against a wall to the side of him. Neither person said a word to Johnny.

"I haven't done anything!" Johnny was definitely on edge.

"Who said you did anything?" questioned Stewart.

"Well," answered Johnny hesitantly. "You're always picking on me."

The phone rang in front of Ms. Stewart. She placed the phone down and walked over to the door. "Come in," said the principal. "Thanks for coming down on such short notice."

Johnny looked up into the face of his dad. His father looked like Johnny in a much bigger version. His red freckles were even brighter than Johnny's. "I've got to get back to work! What's this all about?" He sat down beside Johnny and slapped him in the back of the head. "What have you done this time?"

Johnny winced from the slap. "I haven't done anything," he said in a whine. "They are just picking on me again - like they always do."

Roberts saw the look on Johnny's face, which told him he was working his dad.

Ms. Stewart went on, "This morning one of our students complained that Johnny threw mud and dirty water on her."

"What's a few drops of mud going to hurt?" said Johnny's father. "Kids are going to be kids! He's just a boy. Aren't you making a big deal out of this?"

"It wasn't a few drops," added Mr. Roberts. "It was a bucket of mud and water!"

"Did you do this?" Johnny's father looked at his son with a look that would have scared anyone. There was no possibility that Johnny would ever tell the truth.

"No," said Johnny. "This girl is always trying to get me into trouble. She's telling a lie." Johnny wouldn't look at his dad in the eye. "She probably fell down on her own."

Johnny's father stared at his son. "He's telling me the truth. He knows that if he lied to me that I would give him a good whipping with my belt."

Johnny was trying not to smile. He had his dad on his side. Johnny knew his father would never change his mind, even if he was wrong.

"What are you going to do? Are you going to suspend him from school for something he didn't do?" Johnny's father was becoming more aggressive.

"No," answered the principal. "This did not happen at school. If the girl's parents wish to call the police, they may choose to do so."

"You guys are making a big deal out of this!" shouted Johnny's father to the principal. "You are picking on my kid again!" He pushed back his chair. "I've got to get back to work!" He looked at his son. "You want to stay or go home?"

"I'll stay," said Johnny calmly. "I can't miss some important lessons today." Johnny tried to imitate a model student, but Roberts and Stewart weren't buying it.

"Make sure you are home when I get there." Johnny's father walked out of the office with the same gruffness he walked in with.

Johnny looked at Ms. Stewart and Mr. Roberts faces. "Can I leave?" He was trying hard not to laugh in their faces. "I don't want to be late for class."

"Yes," said the principal. Stewart and Roberts watched Johnny as he left. "That boy is going to get into serious trouble one day, and his father will not be able to ignore it."

Johnny walked out of the office with a big grin on his face. "That's enough for today!" He knew how much fear was in everyone now. Johnny would enjoy watching the fear grow all week. He thought, "Bobby will be the last one I get. Then, we'll see who wins the election!"

Bobby waited outside the front doors after school for Brad, Liz, and Tim. He was surprised that Tim wasn't already there waiting for him. Usually, Tim couldn't wait to get going home and have fun. Bobby saw Brad walking by himself slowly toward him. Brad's eyes were darting back and forth. Bobby was sure that Brad was keeping an eye out for Johnny.

"Hey Brad!" said Bobby. "Have you seen Tim and Liz?"

"They left with their mom a few minutes ago." Brad began walking home. "Tim convinced his mom that he wasn't feeling well. She came and picked up both of them."

"Tim looked fine at lunch, but he was a little quiet." Bobby was wondering what could have happened. "Do you know what was wrong with him?"

"It's called - Johnny!" Brad explained to Bobby what Johnny and his friends had done to Tim in the bathroom. "I've never seen him this scared."

"What will his parents do?" Bobby figured Tim's mom and dad would be very angry.

"He's not going to tell them." Brad looked down at his feet as the walked.

"Why?" Bobby couldn't understand why Tim wouldn't tell his parents.

Brad went on, "Johnny's bragging how he didn't get caught for what he did to Maria. Tim figures Johnny will just lie again." Brad looked behind them to make sure no one was there.

"This is really wrong!" It was one of very few times that Bobby showed any signs of anger. "He has to be stopped once and for all!"

"That's easy for you to say." Brad looked around again. "He always gets away with it."

The two boys walked the rest of the way home without talking. They said goodbye a couple of blocks from Bobby's house. Brad actually started running home. Bobby watched him for a couple of minutes, and then turned to go the rest of the way home alone.

Bobby walked into the house fairly quiet. His mother was in the kitchen, but heard the door close. "Is that you son?" He sat down on the old worn couch.

"Yes," Bobby answered apathetically.

She walked through the doorway with a kitchen towel over her shoulder. "What's wrong?"

Bobby told his mother all the things that Johnny had done earlier in the day. She listened intently as Bobby shared the day with her.

"Johnny will try to get even with me very soon." He looked at his mother. "I'm not afraid of him. I just can't stand what he is doing to my new friends and other people."

"Do you want your father and me to go to school?" She watched for her son's answer.

Bobby thought about it carefully. "No. I have to finish this myself."

"That's fine," added his mother. "But we will not allow anyone to hurt you! If he touches you, we are going to deal with this boy!"

Bobby could see by the look in his mother's eyes that she was very serious.

"How about helping me with dinner?" Bobby's mother smiled down at her son. "I could really use some help."

"Sure." Bobby liked the way his mother could always make everything look better - including tough situations.

Tuesday went by with no problems from Johnny. He either sat in his chair grinning, or walked by students giving them his intimidating look.

Jamal and Bobby enjoyed gym class for the very first time. Mr. Nelson was actually smiling during class. Maybe it was because he finally got all his clothes back - or that he got the message! Whatever the reasons, he stopped blowing the whistle all the time, and actually talked nicely to the kids while they were stretching. Everyone in the class enjoyed the new Mr. Nelson.

Mr. Roberts was absent and had a substitute teacher. The substitute teacher had the class read from their books for the entire class.

Stephanie told Liz, Jamal, and Bobby that Maria still didn't want to come to school.

Liz never said a word about Tim. Maybe, she didn't know. Bobby figured Tim wouldn't tell her because she would go straight to their parents.

Johnny had been extremely successful in intimidating everyone! He walked around with a cocky look and made people get out of his way.

Wednesday morning Bobby met Brad, Tim, and Liz at the corner down the street from his house. Bobby was pleased to see Tim back again. They all walked to school and in the large front doors together. Johnny stepped in front of them as soon as they were in the hallway. "How's it going guys?"

Tim and Brad stepped back away from him.

Johnny stepped right in front of Bobby. His arm was flailing back and forth. "Oh! No!" Johnny spoke in a loud voice. "My stupid pen has leaked again." His grin grew even larger.

Bobby's eyes looked down at his new coat. Splotches of blue ink were all across the front. He looked back up at Johnny angrily. In a split second, he shoved Johnny back three steps with his hands.

Johnny's temper flew immediately, as he jumped back in front of Bobby. "Come on punk!" He held up his fist in front of him. Johnny was clearly trying to start a fight with Bobby. "Think you're tough? Come on!"

Bobby never took his eyes off Johnny. He figured that if he had to fight with Johnny, he would try to hit him as hard as he could in the stomach.

A student walking by shouted, "Ms. Stewart is coming this way!"

Bobby and Johnny looked at the student at the same time. It was Thomas.

Johnny grabbed his things and started walking down the hall in the direction of Ms. Stewart. It only took a few minutes for Johnny to realize that Thomas had tricked him. He thought, "I will get you for that!"

Bobby looked at Thomas, "Thanks."

Thomas never said a word. He held up one finger in front of his face, and then turned and left.

Brad and Tim were still stunned. They could not believe Bobby's anger. Nobody had ever treated Johnny like that.

"Were you nuts?" asked Brad. "He almost got you in a fight!"

Bobby looked down at his new coat. Johnny had no idea what this coat meant to him.

Tim patted Bobby on the shoulder. "We'd better get to class - no sense in letting the jerk think he can bully us forever!" Tim's famous grin had returned.

Brad looked at Bobby and Tim like they were both crazy.

Tim placed one finger up in the air. "The SDL will not be stopped!" The boys hurried down the hallway to class. They wondered what Johnny would be up to when they got there.

Johnny was sitting in Mr. Reed's class waiting for Brad, Bobby, and Tim to walk in. He was enjoying his intimidation of everyone greatly, and figured that he would get after Bobby as soon as possible.

Bobby stopped at the door and looked in. He was glad to see Maria again in her seat across from Johnny. Bobby did not walk down the edge of the room as normal. Instead, he walked directly to Maria's desk, dropped down to one knee in the aisle, and looked at her. His back was to Johnny.

Johnny sat in his desk stunned. He didn't know what to do. Johnny sat there instead, staring at the back of Bobby.

Bobby looked at Maria with a big smile. "I'm glad you're back." He pointed to the front of his coat. "As you can see, I have encountered a little trouble with my clothes as well! Maybe, you and I should start a new fashion."

Maria finally giggled, "It's good to be back!" She looked at his coat with all the blue ink splotches on it. "I like your new look!"

Bobby held up one finger for her to see. "We are one!"

Maria smiled back and nodded her head.

All of a sudden, Bobby seemed to lose his balance - or did he? He fell back right into Johnny and his desk. Johnny flipped backwards to the floor with the desk upside down beside him. Johnny's things went everywhere. Bobby was square on top of Johnny.

"Get off of me!" shouted Johnny. "You did that on purpose!"

Mr. Reed walked over to the tangle of boys and desk. He helped both of them to their feet.

"No, I didn't," said Bobby calmly. "It was an accident."

"That's a lie!" shouted Johnny.

"It was an accident," said Maria. "Bobby was talking to me and lost his balance." She brought up one finger and casually placed it by her cheek.

"It was an accident," said another student. "I saw it too!"

Several students seated nearby said the same thing. It caught Bobby's attention that each of them had one finger pointing up.

"Let me help you," offered Bobby to Johnny. His voice was mocking. "Accidents do happen, as you would well know."

Johnny shoved Bobby away. "Leave me alone!"

Bobby picked up his own things and winked at Maria. His eyes sparkled as he stared at a giant 'B' on the back of Johnny's shirt. It looked like the same ink used on Bobby's coat by Johnny – but how?

Maria's eyes grew large as she saw the letter 'B' on Johnny's shirt. It wasn't long before every kid in the room saw the ink stains - including Mr. Reed. No one said a word.

Bobby walked over to his desk and sat down.

He felt Tim's hand on his shoulder. "Well done!"

Bobby turned toward Brad. "It looks like it is going to be a great day!"

Brad chuckled as well, "I think it is already a great day."

Bobby never saw Johnny after class or the rest of the day. Kids all across the school were talking about the incident in Mr. Reed's classroom. Johnny didn't find out about the ink until lunch. Unfortunately for him, he had to wear the shirt the rest of the day.

Bobby and his friends enjoyed the walk home after school. They said goodbye at the corner. Each of them went home with a smile on their face.

"I'm home!" shouted Bobby as he opened the front door of his house.

Bobby's mother knew from the sound of her son's voice it had been a good day.

"My coat got in the way of some flying ink." Bobby held the coat in front of him. "Do you think we can get it off?"

His mother looked at the ink carefully. "I think it will all come off. You go do your homework and I'll work on it."

"Thanks Mom." Bobby started to walk away. He gave his mom a kiss on the cheek as he passed by.

"How was the day?" asked his mother. She was wondering if there had been any further problems with the bully.

"It was great!" Bobby's happiness was easily heard in his voice. "I need to write a paper for tomorrow." He thought, "The Libertas!"

"I'll call you for dinner." His mother took the coat and began to clean the ink from it.

Bobby went down stairs and turned on the light over the table. He thought, "This issue of the 'Libertas' has to be very special." Bobby sat down on his bed with his back to the wall. He pulled both of his knees close to his chest, as he thought to himself, "It has to be very special."

He picked up his old book on the American Revolution, and thumbed through the pages until his eyes stopped on a letter written July 3, 1776 from Philadelphia, Pennsylvania at the meeting of the Second Continental Congress.

John Adams, who would one day be the second President of the United States, wrote a letter to his wife Abigail. "Yesterday the greatest Question was decided, which ever was debated in America, and a greater perhaps, never was or will be decided among Men. A Resolution was passed without one dissenting Colony 'that these united Colonies, are, and of right ought to be free...'"

Bobby looked up from the book. "Ought to be free!" He scooted off his bed and sat down at the table. Bobby was writing as fast as he could. The words seem to flow from his pen to the paper. Bobby stopped writing after a short time and read his work:

School is a wondrous place to learn about our past and to explore our future; but what good is it, if we forget our past and those around us everyday. School isn't for just one person, it is for all people - it is about being free - free to be educated - free to be safe - and free to be happy. Our forefathers sacrificed everything in the name of freedom. What are we willing to sacrifice in the name of freedom?

Today, there are those among us who would take away our right to be free, to be happy, and to be safe. No longer can we allow these people to intimidate or harm us. It is time to unite as one force and say to these people, 'We will not allow you to do this anymore!'

A time is coming when all of us will be asked to stand up and be counted. That time is now!

Signed the SDL.

Bobby grabbed his letter and ran up the stairs into the kitchen. His father was just walking in from work. "Mom! Dad!" shouted Bobby as he tried to grab breaths of air. "I need to take my letter to Maria's house. It's really important."

He showed the letter to both of his parents. "I'm very proud of you," said his father after he read the letter. "I've got enough gas in the car. We'll drive."

Bobby's mother turned off the stove. "I'm coming too!" She pulled on her coat quickly. "Let's go!"

Bobby and his parents quickly jumped into the car and took off. Bobby had Maria's address on a piece of paper. It wasn't long before they parked in front of a beautiful home. Bobby ran up the sidewalk and knocked on the door.

"The door opened slowly as a woman looked out at Bobby. "May I help you?"

"Hi! I'm Bobby, a friend of Maria's." Bobby stepped closer to the door. "We are working on a project for school together."

"Please step inside," said the woman. "I will go get her."

Bobby stepped inside the nice-looking home and waited by the door. He had never seen a home more wonderful.

"Hey there!" said Maria with a big smile on her face. "What's happening?"

"Would you make one last copy of the 'Libertas'?" Bobby handed Maria his written copy of the letter.

She read the letter carefully then looked up at Bobby. "I will be at the front doors in the morning with the copies." Maria looked back down at the letter. "How will we get the Committee there in the morning?"

Bobby smiled at Maria, as he opened the door of the house. Maria could see both of his parents in the old car outside. "The Sons and Daughters of Liberty will ride tonight!" Bobby waved goodbye. "I'll see you in the morning!" Bobby jumped into the car with his parents. "Jamal's house is next. It is close by."

Bobby ran up to the door. Jamal answered it himself. Bobby told him the plan for the next morning. Jamal volunteered to go to Stephanie's home and Whitney's. Bobby ran back to his car, stopped beside the car door, and looked back at Jamal. Bobby slowly raised one finger in the air.

Jamal raised his finger proudly, as he smiled at Bobby.

Bobby opened the door of the car and sat down. His father drove Bobby to Brad's house, and finally the twins.

Tim answered the door. "What's wrong?"

Bobby explained the plan to Tim. He watched Tim's face light up.

"It's about time!" shouted Tim loud enough for Bobby's parents to hear it in the car.

"I'll see you in the morning." Bobby got back into the car. "Thanks Mom. Thanks Dad. I'm done." Bobby looked at his mother with an apologetic look. "Do you think we can reheat dinner?"

"I'm sure we can," answered his mother.

Bobby sat back in the seat. He thought, "Tomorrow will be our declaration – our freedom!"

CHAPTER 10

Bobby's Story

Bobby and the others were excited to get to school the next morning. There was one day left before the school elections, and there were still things to do. Each of them knew the key to stopping Johnny was winning the election. Maria was standing eagerly at the front door with copies of the 'Libertas' under her coat. All of the Committee seemed to arrive at the same time. Maria gave each one a short stack of papers to post.

"Please give me some!" said a quiet voice. Bobby and the others turned around. Thomas was standing behind them. "Please! Give me some. I will get them out."

Bobby took half of his copies and gave them to Thomas. "Be careful that no one sees you!" He turned back around to the rest of the group. "Try to get them up this morning. We'll all meet after school out in front and review our plan for the assembly." The group broke up and went their different directions. Each person was excited to get the new issue on the walls. Without a doubt, this issue would create a lot of talk around the school.

No one noticed Johnny hiding in a doorway across the hallway. "So this is our famous author of the 'Libertas'. I should have guessed it." Johnny stepped out into the hallway and walked toward Mr. Reed's class. "He's mine!"

The Committee and Thomas worked quickly to get all the copies up on walls and doors. This time there was twice as many. By the time the bell rang, almost every copy was up. Students were already walking down the hallways talking about it.

Bobby walked up to the door of Mr. Reed's classroom several minutes ahead of the bell. He could see that Johnny was in his seat smiling at him. Bobby wondered what was on his mind, but he was sure it wasn't good.

Tim and the others walked up behind him in the doorway. Each of them gave Bobby the look, which told him the 'Libertas' was up everywhere in the school.

Mr. Roberts walked by the boys in the doorway and started talking to Mr. Reed.

Bobby and the others walked down the aisle to their seats. Bobby and Johnny never took their eyes off each other.

No one could hear a word Roberts and Reed said, but both men were reading the new copy of the 'Libertas'. Mr. Roberts said a couple more things to Mr. Reed - then walked out the door. He glanced in Bobby's direction for just a second.

Mr. Reed took his attendance quickly and stood up facing the students. "It seems the author or authors of the 'Libertas' have shared another publication with us." Mr. Reed took the copy Mr.

Roberts brought into the classroom and read from it to the class. "What do you think this is about?"

Johnny quickly spoke out. "It is just a practical joke!" He tried to act like he knew everything about it. "It's just a stupid paper trying to make everyone believe that we have problems at school." Johnny bobbed his head back and forth, trying to act as if he said something very important.

No one said a word in the classroom. Finally, Bobby spoke up, "That must have been what the British said about the thirteen colonies." Bobby stared through Johnny. "They didn't believe there were any problems in America, and never thought the colonists would ever sacrifice themselves for freedom."

Johnny had no clue what Bobby had said, but he was sure that it made him look bad. He turned back around in his chair facing the front of the room.

"What are the things worth sacrificing for today?" asked Mr. Reed.

"Freedom from someone hurting you!" said Tim confidently, as he stared at the back of Johnny's head.

"Freedom from being intimidated and threatened by others." The voice was Thomas in the corner of the room.

Johnny turned his head quickly in Thomas' direction. He thought, "I don't have to put up with this little pipsqueak." Johnny gave him his meanest look. Thomas continued to stare back at him.

"The freedom from someone using words and lies to hurt you!" said another student.

One after another students spoke about acts of meanness. Most of them seemed to fit Johnny. No one wanted to say how to stop it.

Bobby and the others listened intently to the opinions of the students.

"We'll talk more about this next week." Mr. Reed could see trouble coming. He gave everyone a reading assignment and walked around the room monitoring the class. He stopped by Bobby's desk. In a quiet voice, the teacher said, "Your writing style is very different. You might try writing for a newspaper some day." Mr. Reed smiled down at Bobby, "or write a book."

Bobby was sure that Mr. Reed knew he was the author of the 'Libertas'. He watched the teacher for a little bit wondering why he hadn't said anything.

Mr. Reed dismissed the class and reminded everyone the assembly would be tomorrow morning first thing in the gym. He blocked off Johnny from leaving the room. "Are you ready for your speech tomorrow?"

Johnny wanted to follow Bobby and the others, but Reed wasn't about to let him get away. "I guess so."

"I've got a few minutes," said the teacher. "You can practice on me."

"Oh," said Johnny. "I don't want to bother you."

"No bother at all," answered Reed. "We can practice past the bell for a little bit, and then I will walk you to your next class and fix it with the teacher." Mr. Reed gave Johnny is helpful smile. "In fact, I'll pick you up after class and we can practice your speech during lunch."

Johnny could find no way of getting around Mr. Reed, and finally gave in.

Thomas was just leaving the room, and laughed at what Mr. Reed had done to Johnny. "That ought to keep him away from everybody the rest of the day."

Johnny must have read Thomas' mind. He sneaked a hated look at Thomas as he left the room. Thomas knew he had better watch out!

Bobby and the others enjoyed a quiet day from Johnny. It seemed every time Johnny was free; Mr. Reed would take him to his room to practice for the assembly. They met out in front of the school at the end of the day as planned. Everyone wished Bobby good luck at the assembly in the morning.

Suddenly, they heard a siren coming toward the school. A couple kids ran by saying a student was hurt on a bicycle around the corner.

Tim yelled at the kids, "Who is it?"

One of the kids yelled back, "Thomas. He looked dead!"

Tim looked at Bobby and the rest of the group. They started running toward the sound of the siren. Bobby could see a crowd of people circled around something on the ground. The people moved out of the way, as the ambulance backed up.

Bobby worked his way through the people until he could see Thomas lying in the street. Thomas was bleeding from a wound on his head and appeared to be unconscious. Kids standing in the crowd were already gossiping about what had happened. Several were telling their friends that Thomas was dead.

Bobby and the others watched as Thomas was taken away in the ambulance. They listened to the people talking to each other. No one seemed to know how Thomas got hurt.

"How far away is the hospital?" asked Bobby. "I'm going."

"Not too far," answered Tim. "I'll go with you."

Liz agreed to tell Bobby's mother about the accident, and that he went to check on Thomas.

Bobby and Tim ran down the street in the direction the ambulance. They got to the hospital about thirty minutes later. The boys ran into the front lobby and tried to find out how Thomas was doing. The lady at the desk told the boys to sit down, and that she would go find out.

In a few minutes, a tiny woman walked out of the elevator by the doors. She walked up to Bobby and Tim. Her eyes were red from crying, "Are you friends of Thomas? I am his mother."

Bobby's heart sunk to the floor. He wondered if Thomas was really alive. "Yes," answered Bobby quietly. He introduced Tim and himself. Bobby was afraid to ask. His voice quivered, "How is he?"

"Thomas is still unconscious," His mother's voice began to quiver, "he was hurt real bad!" She looked at Bobby. "Do you know what happened to him?"

"I'm sorry," replied Bobby. "We weren't with him when he got hurt."

"Is one of your friends named Johnny?" asked his mother. "Thomas has muttered his name a couple of times."

Tim and Bobby looked at each other. They both wondered if Johnny had done something to hurt Thomas.

"Can I come back in the morning?" asked Bobby. "I'd really like to see him."

"Sure." Thomas' mother smiled warmly. "I'm sure he will be better."

Tim and Bobby hoped she was right. The two walked home without saying much. Both of them were pretty sure that if Johnny was involved, he had gone too far this time. They went home wondering if Thomas was going to live or die.

Bobby walked in the door at home quietly. He looked at his mother and father standing in front of him. Bobby placed his arms around his mother and began to cry. "Thomas shouldn't have been hurt!" The tears seemed like a flood down Bobby's cheeks. "I don't understand why people have to be mean to each other."

Bobby's mother and father finally calmed him down. His mother promised to take him to the hospital in the morning and then to school. Bobby found it very difficult to sleep. He wondered if Thomas was still alive.

The next morning Bobby was up early. He wanted to go to the hospital, but he was scared that he might hear bad news. Bobby looked at his old worn out coat hanging on the wall. He ran his hand over it, and then placed it in a sack. He reached down to the floor and picked up his old shoes with holes in them, and placed them in the sack as well. Bobby walked up the stairs to the kitchen with his old clothes in the sack under his arms.

"What do you have there?" said his mother.

"Just some things to share with my friends," answered Bobby.

Bobby and his mother got into the car and drove to the hospital. They walked into the hospital together. His mother proceeded over to a desk to find out about Thomas. She walked back to Bobby with a smile on her face. "He's getting better. Would you like to say hello?"

"Yes!" Bobby was so excited. "Where's he at?"

"Upstairs," answered his mother. "Let's use the elevator."

Bobby and his mother rode the elevator up two floors. They found Thomas' mother standing outside the room. She looked exhausted, but relieved that her son was going to make it.

Bobby introduced his mother to her. The two seemed to hit it off immediately. Bobby walked into the room by himself. Thomas was lying flat in the bed. His head was bandaged and he was looking out the window. One of his legs was in a large sling hanging over the bed - it was probably broken. Beside the bed was a blue box with numbers on the screen. Bobby figured it was monitoring his heart and other things.

Thomas turned his head slowly toward Bobby. He had two black eyes and a huge bruise on his forehead. Thomas forced a weak smile. "Hi Bobby." Thomas' voice was quiet and weak. "Thanks for coming by."

"No problem." Bobby continued to stare at all the bruises and marks on his body. "How long will you be here?"

"The doctor told me I'll be here for at least three days." Thomas looked down at his leg. "I broke my leg, also!"

"Thomas," asked Bobby softly, "What happened?"

Thomas turned his head toward the window for a moment, then back to Bobby. He sighed, "Johnny knocked me off my bicycle as I rode by!" Thomas' voice grew a little louder. "Johnny was hiding behind some bushes a block from the school. He yelled something at me, and then knocked my bike and me over. That was the last thing I remembered until I awoke here."

"What did your mom do when you told her?" said Bobby.

"You're the only person I've told." Thomas began to cry softly. "He hurt me! I didn't do anything to him!"

Bobby felt his emotions beginning to swell inside. Tears formed in his eyes, as he looked down on Thomas. "You have to tell your mom and even the police. What he did is wrong - very wrong! Johnny must be stopped! You have to let adults deal with this."

"You're right," Thomas nodded his head, "please get my mom."

Bobby walked out to Thomas' mother. She was still talking to his mother. "Thomas needs to tell you how he got hurt."

Thomas' mother walked into the room and sat down beside her son, Bobby and his mother stood by the door, listening to Thomas' story of how Johnny hurt him.

"You have to tell the police what happened!" Thomas' mother was very calm. "This boy can't be allowed to get away with this."

Thomas nodded his head, and then looked at Bobby. "That's what Bobby said to me." He forced a slight smile to Bobby and his mother. "Thanks for coming by."

Bobby couldn't say anything back for a moment. He just felt sad to see how much Thomas had been hurt by Johnny. "I'll come back to see you, as soon as I can."

"Your father and I will bring you back tonight after dinner," said Bobby's mother. "Is that soon enough?"

"Thanks mom," answered Bobby. "Maybe, we can find a game to play around here."

Thomas' mother knew that her son had a great friend. She thanked Bobby and his mother for coming, and looked forward to seeing them after dinner.

Thomas asked Bobby to come closer to him, "Now it's your turn! You go to that assembly and win!"

Bobby looked at Thomas and thought, "The sacrifices made by others in the name of freedom are so great." Bobby smiled back and raised his finger, "The power of one!"

Thomas held up his bruised hand with one finger pointing upward. "Libertas!"

Bobby left with his mother from the hospital. He was completely focused on what he needed to do. There was no fear - only pure determination.

Bobby's mother drove the car up to the edge of the sidewalk in front of the school. She looked up at the front door; Bobby's friends were waiting for him. "She looked at her son, "I'll see you after school. Good luck!"

Bobby stepped out of the car and walked confidently to his waiting friends. He told them everything about Thomas. They were relieved to know that Thomas was going to be okay. Most of them were going to try and see him sometime during the weekend at the hospital.

Jamal looked at Bobby, "It's time to go to the assembly. Are you ready?"

"Yes." Bobby looked at everyone, who had done so much. "Thank you." It was all that he could say.

The group walked into the doors and down the hallway to the gym. The stage was built into the wall and pulled out for special occasions. The students were seated in chairs facing the stage.

Mr. Reed saw Bobby walk in and motioned to him to stand by the side of the stage.

Bobby caught Ms. Stewart by the door and updated her on Thomas' condition.

"Thanks Bobby!" Stewart was pleased to know Thomas would be all right. ""I'll share the good news with everyone."

Bobby walked over to Mr. Reed. Johnny was standing just behind him, and staring at him with his mean grin.

Reed pointed to the stage. "On the stage are five chairs. The middle chair is for the principal, the chairs on both sides of Ms. Stewart are for Mr.

Roberts and me." Reed looked at Johnny. "You will be seated by me."

"...And you will be seated by me." Mr. Roberts walked up to Bobby.

Mr. Reed looked at both boys. "You can only speak for ten minutes - no longer! Are there any questions?" He waited for a second, but no one said anything. "Good! Now let's flip a coin to see who goes first. Heads and Johnny goes first; tails then Bobby goes first." Mr. Reed tossed the coin high into the air spinning. It hit the floor and spun around in circles. Each of them anxiously waited for the coin to stop. Mr. Reed looked down at the coin as it came to a stop, "Heads! Johnny's first."

Ms. Stewart walked up to the microphone and waited for the students to quit talking with each other. "Before we begin our speeches today, I'd like to pass on some information to those of you who are friends of Thomas - he will be okay!" The audience began to clap their hands in relief. "He's hurt pretty bad, but he will get better. We will get information out to your teachers this afternoon, and they will share it with you during classes."

Bobby's dark brown eyes stared at Johnny with determination, as the principal spoke to the audience.

Johnny tried to avoid looking at Bobby. He was sure that Bobby knew what he had done.

"Today is our student elections for president. As you listen to their speeches, ask yourself, who would best represent you and the school. I will ask that we treat both candidates with the respect they deserve. Either Mr. Reed or Mr. Roberts will introduce each candidate. Each candidate will be allowed up to ten minutes to give his speech. This will be followed by elections and the results announced at lunch. Good luck to both candidates."

Stewart invited Mr. Roberts and Mr. Reed to the stage. She waited for the two teachers to walk up the stairs. The students in the audience gave them a polite applause. "And now our two candidates - Johnny and Bobby!" The applause in the gym was incredible.

Johnny walked up the stairs of the stage first with Bobby following. Bobby was still carrying his sack in his arms. The two boys crossed the stage and sat down by their assigned teacher. Johnny was obviously enjoying the power of being on stage.

"The two boys have flipped a coin to see who will go first. Johnny will speak first and Bobby second." The principal reminded the students of their behavior and asked that the lights in the gym be turned down.

Ms. Stewart went to her chair as Mr. Reed walked up to the microphone. "Today, I am proud to introduce our first candidate."

Bobby sat listening to the introduction, as he looked out into the audience. He couldn't see anything but the first couple of rows. In the front row were Tim, Liz, Brad, Jamal, Maria, Stephanie, and Whitney. There was an empty chair between Jamal and Maria. Bobby could see a sign taped to the chair with the word 'Thomas' on it. Each of them was smiling at Bobby. Bobby smiled back.

At the end of the introduction, the audience applauded politely for Johnny. He walked up to the microphone and began part of his speech. The extra time with Mr. Reed had definitely improved his speech - then something changed!

Johnny looked back at Bobby with a sly look, "Lately our school has been disrupted with a newspaper, that nobody knows who the author is; newspapers that accuse people of being bullies. These stories are just lies."

Ms. Stewart, Mr. Roberts, and Mr. Reed looked at each other, wondering where this was going. Jamal and the others in the first row were wondering the same thing.

Johnny puffed up even bigger, "The person responsible for this happening is none other than Bobby! What do you have to say about that?" Johnny turned and grinned at Bobby.

There was a silence in the gym. Everyone was watching for Bobby's reaction. There was none! He sat there with his determined look and said nothing.

"That figures!" Johnny turned back around to the audience "Let me conclude with this," said Johnny triumphantly. He was sure that he had destroyed Bobby once and for all. "I will be president!" He gave the audience a look that said, "You'd better vote for me!"

The audience applauded politely, but only for a few seconds.

Mr. Roberts walked up to the microphone, "A new student walked into our school a short time ago. He very quickly impressed us as teachers and you as students with his caring and understanding. He even made friends with Herman!" The audience laughed hard. "I give you your second candidate - Bobby!"

The applause was more than just polite. Johnny tried to see into the darkness, but couldn't make out who was clapping so hard. There was an excitement building in the air.

Bobby walked up to the microphone and took it off the stand. He held it with one hand. "I would like to tell you a story, and then I will answer my fellow candidate's question." He looked back at Johnny confidently. "First, I want to tell you a story. It's called Bobby's Story!" Bobby walked back to his chair picked up the sack and the chair and returned to the front of the stage. He emptied the contents on the floor, placed his good coat on the back of the chair and sat down.

The audience was perfectly quiet - there was not a sound in the entire gym. Everyone was waiting for his next words.

Bobby unlaced his boots and took them off carefully. He slipped into his old worn out shoes. Bobby picked up the old coat on the floor, stood up, and gently pulled it on. He walked to the front of the stage and looked out into the faces of the students and messed up his hair slightly. He began to speak loud enough for everyone to hear him, "Once upon a time there was a boy named Bobby. He was a great kid that loved to laugh, be happy, and to learn about all the great wonders of the world. Then one day his world came crashing down, when he found out that he had to leave the only home he had ever known. You see - his parents lost their jobs. They had no money to pay the bills and to live on. His family lost everything - their home, their furniture, and their dignity. But it wasn't those things that Bobby missed most of all - it was his friends and family. Those were the people he had known his entire life. They didn't care what he looked like or how nice his home was."

The audience was listening to every word that Bobby said. His friends in the front row were there to support him. Tears began to form in the corners of Maria's eyes.

"Bobby's father and mother told him that they would have to move to the city to find new jobs. His heart was broken as they packed everything they owned into an old car and a small wooden trailer." The audience continued to hang onto each word of the story.

"Bobby and his family moved to the city. At first his father had to work at two jobs just to survive. They found an old broken down house, which was hard to keep warm." Bobby stopped telling the story for a moment and looked around. "His family didn't have much money for decent meals. They ate things like tomatoes and bread, or sometimes - boiled potatoes, gravy, and green beans. Tea was a treat in their house."

An air of sadness started to spread throughout the audience. No one had any idea how hard it had been for him.

Bobby continued with his story as he looked out into the audience. "The boy didn't have nice new clothes. Instead, he wore clothes that had been worn by somebody else before him. His coat was ragged, and his shoes had holes in the sides. The boy was embarrassed as the people looked at him strangely."

Bobby walked up close to the edge of the stage and looked down into the faces of the students. He lowered his head and looked at his toes, as he had done so many times in front of the school.

Maria was remembering the past. She still couldn't believe she had treated him like that. The tears began to trickle from her eyes and down her cheeks.

"The boy looked at his feet because he was embarrassed!" Bobby walked to the side of the stage and back. "Students would walk by and choose not to see him. Others said hurtful things about his clothes and hair."

The audience continued to listen carefully. They had never heard anyone speak like this before.

Mr. Nelson stood against the wall thinking about the past, as he listened to Bobby.

"The boy's parents did without things for themselves, so they could buy their son the things he needed instead." Bobby stared out into the middle of the audience for a moment. "His father walked each day through the snow and cold temperatures – just so his son could have a warm coat and dry feet." Bobby took off the old worn out coat and placed it in one hand. He held the other coat in his other hand. His voice became stronger and stronger, as he moved back to the center of the stage. "He wondered what was different between a boy wearing a new coat and a boy wearing an old coat." Bobby pointed down at his feet with his hand. "He wondered what was different between a boy wearing old shoes and a boy wearing new shoes."

Bobby hesitated for a few moments. "He couldn't understand why people said hurtful things about his clothes. Did they do it because it made them feel better?" Bobby looked out at the audience, "How can you feel better if you hurt someone else?" Bobby turned around to look at Johnny. Johnny looked down at his feet.

"The boy endured being intimidated and threatened. He kept asking himself why he wasn't being allowed to be happy and safe. The boy wondered why adults and students alike weren't trying to make things better. Didn't anyone care?"

Bobby looked down at his friends in front of him. "If one person does something wrong – is the thing they did wrong?" Bobby's friends all nodded their heads in agreement. "Yes. It is wrong." Bobby lifted his eyes to look into the faces of the audience in the back rows. "If twenty people do something wrong – is the thing they did wrong?" He saw more and more people in the audience nodding their heads in agreement. "Yes. It is still wrong." Bobby continued to look out at the different areas of the audience. "If two hundred people do something wrong – is the thing they did wrong?" Bobby could see almost every student in the audience nodding their heads. "Of course it is wrong!" Bobby stood silently for a moment. "Wrong is wrong, no matter how many people do it. It is important that we must stop the thing that is wrong. We must stand up for what is right. It only takes one person to speak out for what is right – the power of one!"

Bobby held up one finger in the air. Everywhere across the audience students began to hold up one finger. "This story isn't ending – it is just beginning!" Bobby looked behind him. Johnny was still looking down at his feet, but Ms. Stewart, Mr. Reed, and Mr. Roberts were each holding up one finger. Bobby turned back around to the audience.

"This election isn't about the usual kid stuff! It is about big stuff - stuff like freedom to be happy and safe! It is about how we treat each other and solve our problems. Johnny has asked the question if I am the writer of the 'Libertas'? The answer is yes!"

The gym was silent. Johnny looked up thinking Bobby had finally messed up.

A voice from the front row shouted loudly, "Sons and Daughters of Liberty stand and be counted!" The voice sounded a whole lot like Tim.

Bobby looked down at each of his friends, as each one stood up in the front row. One by one, students across the entire gym began to stand up. Soon, almost every student in the gym was standing.

Mr. Reed looked at Bobby proudly and began to clap his hands. The gym was a thunderous applause. Bobby looked down at his friends with a big grin on his face. He held up his finger one last time, and returned to the side of Mr. Roberts.

Mr. Roberts leaned over to Bobby, "Great job!"

Mr. Reed walked over to Bobby and congratulated him. "I really do like your writing style!" He winked at Bobby and went back to his chair.

Ms. Stewart walked up to the microphone and waited for the audience to quiet down. She waited patiently for the last person to stop clapping.

"Ms. Stewart?" said a voice loudly from the front row of the audience. Jamal was standing up.

"Yes?" answered the principal.

"Our election rules say a voice count can be used at the assembly, but only if the vote is significant for one candidate," said Jamal as held the election rules sheet in his hands. "I would like to invoke that rule."

Ms. Stewart looked back at Mr. Reed. Mr. Reed nodded his head in approval. The principal looked at the audience. "I will ask each of you to vote by calling out the name of your favorite candidate. I will begin with Johnny."

There were scattered voices across the gym.

"Bobby?" said Stewart.

"Bobby! Bobby!" was shouted so loud, that it echoed off the walls of the gym.

Ms. Stewart held her arms up to quiet the group. "You have made your decision. May I present to you - your next President - Bobby!"

Every student and teacher in the gym stood up and applauded. Bobby waved at his friends in the front row. He turned around to thank Ms. Stewart, Mr. Reed, and Mr. Roberts.

Bobby saw Johnny standing off the stage by the doorway talking to a police officer. The officer held Johnny by the arm and escorted him out of the gym. "Wrong is wrong." thought Bobby.

Jamal and the others ran up to the stage to join Bobby. They were so excited. Tim was jumping up and down. Liz was trying to hold him down, but it wasn't working.

Bobby wiped away the tears on Maria's cheeks and smiled at her. "Thanks." Maria smiled back even bigger.

Mr. Roberts walked up to the group. "What's next Mr. President?"

A huge grin spread across Bobby's face, "Basement Tag!"

About

J. Richard Knapp

J. Richard Knapp was born in the Pacific Northwest in a small rural community beside the banks of the great Snake River in the fall of 1949. It was one of those communities where everyone knew each other, and often worked side by side picking fruit to be sent by train to New York City, Chicago, or even Boston. Everyone was either picking fruit or packaging it to be sent by train somewhere in America.

The stories told by Knapp often reflect his experiences as a young boy in this small community exploring the banks of the large river and his community with his closest friends. His adventurous nature and creative mind often led to great tales of the river and fantasies enjoyed by all.

In the early 1960's the United States allowed fruit from Asia to be sold in America for the first time. The small community on the banks of the Snake River could not compete in this new world market. As the months passed by, they could not find any place to sell their fruit. Eventually, apples were left unpicked or rotting on the ground. Workers began to lose their jobs. Small businesses were forced to close their doors forever. Families had to sell everything they owned and move away in hopes of finding work elsewhere. The trains stopped coming.

Knapp's parents soon found themselves without jobs and no future. They sold everything they owned and moved to a nearby city in hopes of starting over again. The months and years ahead were hard, as the family struggled in deep poverty just to survive. Knapp's book, *Bobby's Story*, is based upon this time in his life.

J. Richard Knapp graduated from high school in 1967. His accomplishments as an athlete earned him a scholarship to college, where he earned his Bachelor of Arts Degree, Master of Arts Degree, and a pre-doctorate. He has spent the past thirty two years as a writer, elementary teacher, administrator, graduate school instructor, and recognized leader in education. Knapp has served as a member of the International Symposium on Education with leaders from Great Britain, Japan, Canada, China, Germany, Australia, and the United States of America. Additionally, he has lobbied for schools and youth both in Congress and in his home state of Oregon for over a decade.

J. Richard Knapp lives with his wife of thirty two years in a small community along the banks of the beautiful Umpqua River in western Oregon. He continues to share his stories with children everywhere, and tells them about his adventures along the banks of the great Snake River.

To order copies of the book

Bobby's Story

$12.95 + 2.50 (S&H)

online at:
http://www.BooksToBelieveIn.com/BobbysStory.php

by phone:
have your credit card handy and call:
(303) 794-8888

by fax:
(720) 863-2013

by mail: send check payable to:
Thornton Publishing, Inc.
17011 Lincoln Ave. #408
Parker, Colorado 80134

If it is temporarily sold out at your favorite bookstore,
have them order more of ISBN: 0-9774761-7-0

Name: _____

Address: _____

_____

Phone: _____

E-mail: _____

Credit Card #: _____

Card Type: _____   Expiration Date: ___/ ___

Security Code: _____